"Sorry." He jumped back, his hands out. "I didn't mean to startle you."

His grin said otherwise. He reached past her, opened a drawer, and pulled out a hammer.

"You have tools in the kitchen?" Amanda couldn't resist asking.

"Sure, it's called a tool drawer." His quick wink sent her heart pounding.

He turned and walked out through the dining room to the deck. She held her hand over her heart to slow its beating, glad Linda stood behind her at the sink and couldn't see. No sense in letting everyone witness her infuriating responses to Chad.

"Amanda." Linda's voice was soft but firm. "Maybe this isn't a good idea."

"What?" She turned and looked at Linda with wide, innocent eyes. At least she hoped she looked innocent. "Do you want me to work on the counters first?"

"That isn't what I mean, and you know it. Go ahead and sweep, but tell me something. Do you have feelings for Chad?"

D0667776

MILDRED COLVIN is a native Missourian with three children, one son-in-law, and two grandchildren. She and her husband spent most of their married life providing a home for foster children but now enjoy babysitting the grandchildren. Mildred writes inspirational romance novels because in them the truth of God's presence, even in the midst of trouble, can be portrayed. Her desire is to continue writing stories that uplift and encourage.

Books by Mildred Colvin

HEARTSONG PRESENTS

HP435—Circle of Vengeance—as M. J. Conner
HP543—Cora
HP591—Eliza
HP634—This Child Is Mine
HP643—Escape to Sanctuary
HP707—Mariah's Hope—as M. J. Conner
HP735—Deborah
HP779—Joanna's Adventure
HP929—Facing Tessa's Past
HP946—Redeeming Sarah's Present

Don't miss out on any of our super romances. Write to us at the following address for information on our newest releases and club information.

Heartsong Presents Readers' Service
PO Box 721
Uhrichsville, OH 44683

Or visit www.heartsongpresents.com

Building
Amanda's Future

Mildred Colvin

Heartsong Presents

To extraordinary foster parents who give more than meets the eye to make a difference for good in the lives of children. Especially to Kathy Bowman, a fellow foster parent who went out of her way to serve others. We miss you, Kathy.

A note from the Author:
I love to hear from my readers! You may correspond with me by writing:

Mildred Colvin
Author Relations
PO Box 721
Uhrichsville, OH 44683

ISBN 978-1-61626-374-4

BUILDING AMANDA'S FUTURE

Copyright © 2011 by Mildred Colvin. All rights reserved. Except for use in any review, the reproduction or utilization of this work in whole or in part in any form by any electronic, mechanical, or other means, now known or hereafter invented, is forbidden without the permission of Heartsong Presents, an imprint of Barbour Publishing, Inc., PO Box 721, Uhrichsville, Ohio 44683.

Scripture taken from the HOLY BIBLE, NEW INTERNATIONAL VERSION®. NIV®. Copyright © 1973, 1978, 1984, 2010 by Biblic, Inc.™ Used by permission. All rights reserved worldwide.

Scripture quotations are taken from the King James Version of the Bible.

All of the characters and events in this book are fictitious. Any resemblance to actual persons, living or dead, or to actual events is purely coincidental.

Our mission is to publish and distribute inspirational products offering exceptional value and biblical encouragement to the masses.

PRINTED IN THE U.S.A.

one

Amanda Wilson knelt on the soft, thick lawn beside the tombstone and placed a spray of forget-me-nots against the cool marble. She took a deep breath, letting the scent of fresh-cut grass fill her senses while the early May sun warmed her skin.

With her finger, she traced the words engraved in the stone. JEFFREY ALLEN WILSON. BELOVED SON AND HUSBAND. WE MISS YOU. Such impersonal words to convey the love and loss she could never regain.

She lifted her face toward the blue sky. "Oh Jeff, I do miss you, even though our life together seems more like a dream with each passing year."

She closed her eyes for a moment. "I finished college. That's the good news. The bad news is I'll be teaching in Litchfield, so I have to move home to Illinois."

A sigh escaped as she settled back against her heels. "I'll be staying with Mom and Dad."

She brought her gaze back to Jeffrey's name. "At least it's only temporary, until I get my own place. Anyway, I couldn't leave California without saying good-bye."

She shifted her position, moving closer to a small grave beside her husband's and placed a bouquet of baby's breath in the vase set in front of the marble slab. Tears blurred her vision as she read the engraving. CHARITY FAITH WILSON. GOD'S LOVE BROUGHT YOU INTO OUR LIVES FOR SUCH A SHORT TIME.

A sob escaped before Amanda could hold it back. She held a tissue to her eyes then covered her trembling lips. Five years since she held her tiny daughter. The hurt was no longer fresh and constant as it had once been, but leaving Charity's grave would be hard.

"My precious baby, I miss you so much. I love you, Charity. I always will."

Amanda stood and looked from one stone to another. She and Jeffrey had married much too quickly and for all the wrong reasons. Still, she'd grown to love him and would miss him for the rest of her life. Sometimes little Charity seemed a distant memory brought real by the empty ache in her arms. An ache that would never ease because her arms would never hold another child of her own.

"Good-bye, Jeffrey. Good-bye, Charity," she whispered before turning on her heel and making her way across the cemetery to her car. Time to go home.

She turned the ignition key and let the engine warm while she took one last look at the stones sitting side by side across the cemetery. In her imagination she sensed Jeffrey and Charity urging her to get on with her life.

A sigh escaped. Why Litchfield? Sometimes it was so hard to know if the turning points in life were God ordained or only a cruel twist of life. She put the gearshift in drive and rolled out of the cemetery.

She approached Santa Monica Boulevard and impulsively turned on her right blinker to go west. She hadn't been to the beach for a long time and today was for good-byes. The street stopped at Ocean Avenue with a beautiful view of the beach and palm trees standing so tall and regal with the blue of the ocean and sky stretching beyond as if without end. She drove down to the beach and parked, then walked through the sand remembering the times she and Jeff had played with Charity here.

Charity had loved to sift her fingers through the sand. Memories that had soothed her before now hurt because she'd leave them all behind in the morning. She had picture albums to remember the good times, but for today the loss overwhelmed her. She went to her car and drove back the way she'd come.

The light changed to red as she approached the corner of Ocean Avenue and Santa Monica Boulevard. As she waited for the light, a thought occurred to her. She was sitting at the end of Historic Route 66, a special road that stretched from Chicago to where she now sat in California. Tessa Donovan, in Amarillo, lived near the midpoint, and Sarah Nichols lived in Chicago where the road began. While connected by their friendship, the three of them were also connected by the Mother Road. So, if she drove home, this is where she'd start her journey, and she could stop and visit with each along the way.

The idea was tempting, even though she didn't intend to go as far as Chicago. Yet if she did, she could say she had traveled Route 66 from one end to the other. Of course, she'd be on the road for several days even with the faster interstate freeways that now covered so much of the original highway. The thought of driving across the country on freeways sent a shudder, especially strong after her visit to the cemetery, down Amanda's backbone.

With trembling fingers, she turned on the radio and welcomed the soft music that flowed from the speakers, relaxing her. She drove home for the last night in her apartment. Everything she owned had already been sold or given away, including the car she now drove. Tomorrow, Jeff's parents would take her to the airport where she'd catch a flight to Illinois.

ﾑ

After disembarking at the Springfield, Illinois, airport, Amanda rented a car for the last leg of her journey. As she merged onto Interstate 55 going south out of Springfield, she saw a road sign announcing Historic Route 66. She smiled. California didn't seem so far away now. On a whim, she picked up her cell phone and punched in a familiar number.

When Tessa answered, Amanda said, "Hey, guess where I am."

"Illinois?"

"Yes, but I mean more specific. I'm on your favorite road just south of Springfield."

"Oh, Route 66. Be careful. You can meet some very strange people on that road." She giggled and a male voice rumbled in the background.

"Who was that? Blake?" Amanda smiled at the obvious happiness in her friend's voice.

Tessa laughed. "Yes, my dear husband's objecting to being called strange. I've tried to tell him, if the shoe fits. . ."

Amanda laughed with her and ignored the tiny poke of envy in her heart. While she drove ever closer home, she and Tessa talked and laughed until Tessa had to go. Amanda hung up with a smile. After their short conversation, she felt more relaxed about her move. Her next call was to her parents. They should be home from work by now.

Mom answered.

"Hi. I'm about home, Mom."

"Amanda, we could've met you at the airport. Or Karen could have."

In so many words, she could've let them know her arrival time. Amanda laughed. "Maybe that's why I didn't tell you. I wanted to rent a car, anyway. It's fine, Mom. I'll be there in a few minutes. Okay?"

After they hung up, she tossed her cell phone in the other seat and turned the radio on in time to catch a weather report. Most of central Illinois was under a tornado watch until six o'clock that evening. Music replaced the urgent message as if the announcement was of no importance.

Amanda leaned forward to look up. A blanket of dark gray clouds she hadn't noticed before now covered the sky.

The clock on the car's dash said five thirty. Thankfully, the tornado watch would be over in half an hour, about the time she reached home. Surely nothing would happen. The sky didn't look bad to her. To further ease her mind, the clouds above thinned and a patch of blue appeared, sending sunshine streaking across the land.

She entered Litchfield's city limits. The blue sky dominated the expanse above with only scattered puffs of dark clouds as a reminder of what could have been.

Amanda stopped in the drive of the rambling old house she'd grown up in. The two-story white frame home had been built a hundred years ago. The swing hanging at the end of the wide, welcoming front porch creaked as a breeze pushed it. *Thank You, Lord, for a place to call home.* A happy place.

She sat a moment before releasing her seat belt. She had much to thank God for. Love of family ranked at the top.

She stepped from the car into sunshine.

"I'm so glad you made it safely." Mom met her at the front door. "Did you know we're under a tornado watch?"

Amanda returned her mother's hug. "Yes, but I think it's blown over now."

"Do you need help unloading?" Dad asked.

"No." Amanda gave him a quick hug and lifted her small bag. "Here's what I need for the night. I can get the rest tomorrow."

"That will work. Come on in and tell us what you've been up to." Dad ushered them into the living room.

Amanda told about her uneventful flight and said, "I rented a car rather than bother Karen. I'm sure she's at work or was when we landed."

"Probably." Mom shrugged. "I could've taken off work to

pick you up, but maybe it's best this way. How long will you keep the car?"

"Not long. I'd like to buy my own."

"Until then, you might as well borrow mine and save the rental fee. Dad's been taking me to work here lately, anyway." Mom stood. "I need to check on supper. Why don't you come with me?"

Dad glanced toward the door. "If you ladies will excuse me, I've got a baseball game I'd like to watch."

Amanda smiled at them and shook her head. "Don't start babysitting me. What I'd really like to do, unless you need help, is check out my room before supper."

"If you're sure."

"I'm sure."

Mom headed toward the kitchen, and Dad went to the family room and the TV.

With her overnight bag dropped on the floor of her old room upstairs, Amanda sank to the bed and fell back with her arms outstretched. The muffled sound of the sports announcer on TV in the family room directly below her rose to her room. Dad was watching a baseball game. She laughed and shook her head. Some things never changed. He always watched the sports channel before supper.

The muted sound of the phone ringing brought Amanda from her bed and down the stairs. She followed her mother's voice to the kitchen.

"Hi, Karen. Yes, she got home a few minutes ago. No, there were a few storm clouds, but they cleared off."

Amanda got a drink of water from the refrigerator. She sipped her drink while listening to her mother's side of the conversation with her older sister. Her fingers tightened on the glass when her mother's eyes widened and a sharp gasp left her lips.

"What is it?" Amanda asked.

Mom shook her head. "Were there any injuries?" She listened a moment, and then closed her eyes. "Lord, help them."

"Mom?" Amanda set her glass on the counter as her mother hung the receiver back on the hook. "What's happened?"

Dad stepped out of the family room. "What's going on? Who was that on the phone?"

"Karen. She said Lakeland was hit by a tornado. They don't know the extent of damage yet or how many are injured. But that isn't all of it. A second tornado was sighted, and it's also headed straight for Lakeland."

"How can that be?" Amanda looked out the window at the calm sunshine. Lakeland was fifteen miles away. It didn't seem possible that the sky above Litchfield held only a few dark clouds that appeared to be moving away while tornadoes battered the neighboring town.

Dad held his hand out, gesturing for them. "Let's go in the family room where we can pray. We don't know how bad it is, but God knows."

Amanda knelt with her parents on the carpet in front of the sofa. She bowed her head and listened to her father's strong voice petition the Lord to protect their neighbors in Lakeland. She added her pleas as tears of concern and sympathy fell.

Before they finished praying, the phone rang again. Amanda continued to pray while her mother answered. A few minutes later she came back into the room and sank into the easy chair beside the sofa with her head bowed.

"That was Karen again. She says the tornado has passed and most of downtown Lakeland is leveled. It's on the local station if you want to listen."

Dad pulled himself to his feet and crossed the room to the radio. They listened to the damage report of their neighboring town. Five minutes later he turned the radio off.

The small town of less than two thousand in population had been hit hard. Most of the business district located on the north side of town was gone. Several homes were destroyed. Outlying farms had been leveled. Both tornadoes followed a similar path, the second taking what the first left. At least two lives had been lost, but the radio announcer said the number could rise as reports continued to come in.

Amanda sat with her parents in stunned silence. To think only moments ago her greatest concern was moving back home with her parents for a few months. Her problems seemed so childish now. At least she had a roof over her head.

꙳

Chad Randall turned away from Lakeland Cemetery. The short drive into town didn't take long. He slowed his truck at the city limits to creep down the only cleared main street in the north side of Lakeland. If the heavy traffic was any indication, every thrill seeker in central Illinois was creeping along in front of him. Anger toward the insensitive curiosity of man tore through his heart. Why didn't they stay at home and let these people grieve in private?

Trees looked as if a giant wood shredder had chewed on the top branches, leaving bare, torn trunks in its wake. Foundations held floors of clutter with no walls. Broken glass and bricks covered the ground everywhere he looked.

At the intersection he turned south, leaving the devastation behind. As he drove past untouched buildings and houses, he marveled at the power of the wind. Marveled and cursed it for taking his little sister.

He turned into the parking lot of the state and county offices and stopped near the building. He stepped out of his truck, locked it, and went inside. The receptionist took him to a small private room that held a desk with two chairs facing it. He sat in one to wait for the social worker. When she entered the room, he rose.

"Hello, I'm Mrs. Carter. Mr. Randall?"

He nodded. "Chad Randall."

"Thank you for coming today. I've been working with your niece's case and will help you any way I can."

He shook her hand and sat back down as she took the chair behind the desk.

"Mr. Randall, first I want to tell you how sorry I am for your loss," she began.

He fought the anger and pain that rose to the surface every time he thought of his sister and, rude though it might be, he could not acknowledge her sympathy.

"Your niece is being cared for in a local foster home—"

"That's why I'm here." He cut into her planned speech. "My sister and brother-in-law wanted me to take her if anything happened to them. I'm all she has now. If you'll tell me where she is, I'm prepared to get her."

Mrs. Carter held up a hand. "Mr. Randall, I'm sure you will gain custody of your niece in time. Before we discuss that, I'd like to ask you some questions."

Chad's stomach clenched as he stared at the woman. Why did the government always have to make everything so difficult? "What do you need to know? Character references?"

Mrs. Carter smiled. "I'm not accusing you of being an unfit uncle, but I would like to know where you intend to live. I understand you are Kara's closest living relation?"

Chad nodded. "Yes, my father died while I was in elementary school. My mother passed away a couple of years ago. Steve was raised in foster care. I don't know what happened to his parents. I'm not sure he ever knew his biological father."

"I see." Mrs. Carter glanced at the folder in front of her

and made a notation. She met his gaze again. "The other day on the phone you mentioned you would be staying on your sister's farm so you could rebuild. Have you seen the property yet?"

"No, I got here as soon as I could. I came straight here after the funeral."

"I can sympathize that your concern is with your niece, but rest assured, she's in good hands. The family she's with has two teenage girls who love babies." Mrs. Carter laughed. "She has the equivalent of three mothers fussing over her."

"Ma'am, with all due respect, they aren't her family. She doesn't know them."

Mrs. Carter nodded. "Yes, that was true at first, but she's been there three days, since the night of the storm. Small children adapt quickly. Will you be staying at the farm?"

Chad nodded. She had a point. He didn't even know if he'd have shelter other than his truck. "What do I have to do to get custody of Kara?"

"Since you will likely need a lawyer for probate, may I suggest that you begin proceedings with an attorney to obtain legal guardianship after you've had some time to see what you're up against with the house? Go out and look things over. If you need help cleaning up and rebuilding, go to the courthouse and get on the list. I understand volunteers are being assigned work locations." She looked down at the file again. "You teach at a high school in the northern part of the state, is that correct?"

"Yes, in Rockford."

"I assume you have a home there?"

"An apartment. I live alone. There hasn't been need for a house, but if that's what it takes, I'll buy a house. I intend to raise Kara just as Jessica and Steve wanted." She needed to understand. "Steve might have been raised in foster homes, but he didn't let his background keep him down. As an attorney, he saw the need to provide for his family. I'll check with the firm. I'm sure he made provisions for Kara."

Mrs. Carter smiled. "It sounds as if Steven Jones was one of the rare successes that come out of the foster care system. I always love to hear of those."

"He was a good man." Chad felt his throat tighten and didn't say more.

"I'm sure he was." Mrs. Carter stood and so did Chad. "We'll get this all ironed out, but for now, why don't you take a look at the farm?"

"In the meantime, may I see Kara?"

"Absolutely. Let me call the Warners and set up a visit. Check back with me in the morning. We should know something then."

Chad bit his tongue to keep from saying what he thought of the delay. He wanted to see Jessica's baby now. Rather, he wanted to take Kara home with him. His grief had been so intense that he'd barely thought of his niece beyond his need to get to her.

He again shook hands with the social worker and left. He drove back to the center of the destruction and stopped at the four-way stop. This time he turned to the right—the opposite direction from the way he'd come into town—and drove four miles into the country before turning on the gravel road that led to what was left of his sister's home.

He stopped near the house. For a few minutes he sat in silence and stared out the windshield. The house still stood. So many houses in town had been leveled to the floors with no loss of life. He'd been told that Jessica and Steve had not died in the house. The neighbor who found them assumed that after the first storm passed, Steve went out to take a look at the damage to the barn. Jessica heard on the radio that another tornado was headed toward them and ran out to tell him to take cover. Before they reached shelter, the second tornado hit and flying debris from the barn killed both of them. The house didn't appear to have been touched.

He stepped from the truck and took a quick look around. The barn was little more than a pile of rubble. He walked around the house. Several windows had been shattered. In the backyard, he stopped and stared. A large maple tree leaned against the house with one branch buried in the roof.

Inside he found that not one room would be suitable to shelter a child. He might as well do what the social worker said and get on the list for help. Jessica wouldn't want her baby with strangers. Steve wouldn't want his daughter raised in foster care. The sooner he had help, the sooner he could make a home for Kara.

two

The day after the storms, Pastor Walt Mattson stood before his Wednesday evening congregation with a special plea for help. "Folks in Lakeland have been hit hard. Four people lost their lives in two tornadoes that ripped through the town. Many are without homes while others begin the seemingly impossible task of cleaning up and rebuilding. We've prayed for them, but we can't stop there. Until you see the destruction a tornado leaves, you can't imagine what these people face."

He motioned to the ushers in back. "Gentlemen, if you will start the sign-up sheets circulating, I'll explain a practical, hands-on way we can help."

Amanda sat with her parents and listened. "Churches and civic organizations are asked to provide volunteer workers to help the citizens of Lakeland and the surrounding area rebuild. Of course they need carpenters and plumbers, but their immediate need is workers who can pick up brush and bricks or wood pieces. I can't begin to list the debris scattered everywhere. If you are an able-bodied man or woman and have any free time, please consider donating a few hours to this worthy project. I'm hoping to take a crew of at least five or six from our church this Saturday. We'll be assigned an area and will likely work together."

Amanda took the sign-up sheet and wrote her name on the list. She understood the hollowness of loss. Her heart ached in sympathy. Their homes gone or damaged within moments. Others had lost even more through death.

&.

Saturday morning, Amanda drove her rental car to Lakeland in a caravan of two other vehicles. Linda Maddox rode in the front with her while an older couple sat in the backseat. Linda's daughter Sarah was Amanda's best friend from high school, and Linda had always been a second mother to her.

As they neared Lakeland, signs of damage came into view, but nothing seemed especially devastating until they turned off the highway and drove into the populated area just past the city limits sign.

"Oh, will you look at that?" the woman in the backseat said.

Amanda shuddered at the destruction on either side of the road as she followed the pastor's dark blue sedan. Thankfully the street had been cleared, but she didn't need much imagination to see that piles of bricks, shards of glass, and pieces of buildings on either side had, only days ago, covered the pavement where they now drove.

Some houses suffered roof damage, while many more littered the area up to the edge of the street. On one corner, a floor without walls held nothing except a bathtub and toilet. From her car, Amanda saw a roll of toilet paper sitting between the fixtures even as Linda gasped.

"I've heard of tornadoes doing things like that, but I've never seen it before. How could the wind totally remove an entire house, yet leave something as light as a roll of paper sitting on the floor?"

Amanda shook her head. "I don't know. I'm amazed there weren't more deaths here. Only four people died and a few injuries were reported, yet we've already driven past at least a dozen totally destroyed houses."

A group of people worked by the side of the street, sorting through the mess as they loaded pickup trucks with trash to be hauled away. Amanda itched to stop the car and get out to help. There was so much to do and so few working. How would the town ever be cleaned up?

A brief stop at the county courthouse gave them their assigned location. After driving a few miles into the country, they turned onto a gravel road for a short distance before stopping at a house that appeared to be untouched.

Amanda shared a look and a shrug with Linda as they got out of the car. She closed the driver's door and stood for a moment taking in the peaceful scene. The one-story ranch-style house looked well taken care of. A couple of wooden slat chairs sat on the inviting front porch with a small matching table between them as if waiting for company. The soft green of the house blended harmoniously with the manicured lawn. A flagstone walk curved from the driveway to the front steps.

To the left, several feet back from the house, a cement floor, collapsed walls, and rubble marked the place where a barn once stood. The wind had been selective in its destruction. There, the ground held evidence of its fury.

"Good morning." Pastor Mattson's greeting brought Amanda's attention to the others gathered in a group near the house. "I'm Walt Mattson, pastor of Community Church in Litchfield. This is John Sinclair, Rick Harrison, and Ron Kimbel."

He continued calling off names, but Amanda stopped listening as her gaze focused on the man who moved among the helpers shaking hands and smiling as the workers were introduced.

Her heart skipped a beat before pounding furiously when she recognized who they would be working for. What had it been? Thirteen years? Fifteen? No, she couldn't fool herself into believing she didn't remember. Fourteen years and seven months ago her heart had been broken by the very man who now stood across the yard watching her.

"And Amanda Wilson, who is still leaning against her car. Come on, Amanda, and join us. This young man is Chad Randall. He will be showing us what needs to be done."

Amanda pushed away from the car and circled the group to stand beside Linda, as far from Chad as she could get. Her heart thundered in her ears until she couldn't hear what he or the pastor said. She sought the calming effect of nature in the peaceful scene of several cows grazing across the fence. Taking several deep breaths, she questioned what was happening. *Lord, why of all the places needing help, did You send us here?* What was Chad doing here, anyway? He'd married and moved away. Of course, so had she, but that was different. He should have stayed away.

"We'll be glad to help you any way we can." Pastor Mattson's voice again penetrated Amanda's befuddled brain. He turned to the women in the group. "Ladies, as you can see, the yard there by the barn has enough broken limbs and lumber to keep us all busy. Chad says a large tree in the backyard fell against the house during the storm. He's been unable to remove it without help. For today, would you mind working in the yard, picking up usable lumber and firewood while we men concentrate on removing the tree?"

Elva Harrison gasped and covered her mouth before saying, "Oh my, did the tree do a lot of damage?"

Chad sent the hint of a smile toward the older woman. "Not as much as it could've. A branch broke through the peak of the roof, but didn't touch the attic floor."

His gaze shifted to Amanda as if speaking to her. "My niece's bedroom is directly under the trunk of the tree. If I have anything to be thankful for in all of this, it's that the tree stopped when it did. She was in her bed when it fell."

Amanda couldn't tear her gaze from his. In that moment, time became irrelevant as their past fell away and her heart ached with his pain. At the mention of his niece, she understood his loss. He'd had only one sibling. Jessica. Had she married her high school sweetheart? Were they the man and woman who had died here? Jessica and Steven. Jessica with her laughing blue eyes and dark brown hair so like Chad's. At one time she and Amanda expected to be sisters. The work project became personal as she shared Chad's grief.

A soft smile touched his lips before he looked away, breaking contact with her.

The men began moving toward the backyard. Amanda nodded at a truck in the driveway. "I see a wheelbarrow sticking up in the back of Brother Kimbel's truck. I'll get my gloves from my car; then I'll lift it out. Did you all bring gloves?"

The two older ladies, Mable Kimbel and Elva Harrison, wore long-sleeve shirts tucked into their blue jeans. They each had on wide-brimmed hats to cover their gray hair and shade their faces. Mable wiggled her gloved hands and smiled. "I'm ahead of you, Amanda."

Elva nodded. "Yes, you two girls get your gloves and let's get to work."

Linda, who was the same age as Amanda's mother, whispered as she and Amanda hurried to the car. "Being with those two sweet ladies makes me feel young again."

Amanda laughed. "I know, but I have a feeling we'll be putting out some effort to keep up with them."

She heard a chain saw revving on the other side of the house. "I didn't know anyone brought a saw."

"I don't think they did. It was probably already here." Linda pulled her gloves on and headed toward the barn.

Amanda hurried to catch up. A cold chill chased up her back as she thought of Chad trying to cut through a large tree by himself. He could have been hurt. She shouldn't care. But she wouldn't want anyone hurt, not even Chad.

Elva and Mable had already started dragging broken tree

branches into a pile by the barbed-wire fence separating the yard from the pasture. While they did that, Amanda and Linda made piles of usable lumber near the cement floor that had been the barn. Most were useless for anything other than firewood and those pieces went into the wheelbarrow to deposit across the yard.

"I wonder how far away pieces of this barn are scattered?" Amanda asked.

Linda stretched her back as she looked across the now peaceful countryside with grazing cattle and a cloudless blue sky. "Probably not so far, but on the other hand, part of it could have gone for miles before falling back to the ground. It's hard to tell, isn't it?"

"Yeah, sort of like some of the mistakes we make in life." Amanda watched Chad walk around the end of the house. "Mistakes cause damage. Sometimes far-reaching, sometimes not so far."

Linda followed her line of vision. "Chad Randall. He's grown into a fine-looking man. Is he one of those mistakes you're talking about?"

Amanda turned her back to Chad, covered her face with her hands, and then peeked through her fingers at Linda. "You remember."

Linda laughed. "Of course I remember." She held her finger and thumb together without touching. "You and Chad were this close to getting married. Next thing I knew, you vamoosed to California and the wedding was off. Before your exit dust settled, you'd married someone else. Sarah never did tell me the particulars. Did she know?"

Amanda shook her head. "No."

She tossed more wood on the wheelbarrow, working frantically for several minutes. Linda worked alongside her without pressing the issue. Finally she stopped.

"All right. Keep your secrets. I wasn't asking, anyway." She put her hands on her hips, breathing hard. "Let's not try to finish the entire yard in the next ten minutes, okay? Maybe you can keep up with our elderly friends, but I can't."

Amanda straightened with a broken length of wood in her hand. "I'm sorry, Linda. It's just seeing him again. I mean I didn't know he was anywhere within a hundred miles of here and there he stood looking. . ." She closed her eyes for a moment. When she opened them a tear hovered on her lashes and she brushed it away. She whispered the one word. "Vulnerable. He looks so sad and I want to cry for him." She gave a short, harsh laugh. "He broke my heart and I feel sorry for him."

Linda's voice was soft, sympathetic. "Can you do this?"

"Work for Chad?" Amanda nodded. "Sure. I'll keep my distance and we'll get along fine."

Linda lifted her eyebrows. "Didn't the pastor say we are sent to help clear the destruction, but maybe for another purpose, too? Maybe Chad has a need that our church can reach. Maybe you need to reach out and let God heal all these old hurts. Maybe that's why you're here at this exact moment."

Amanda tossed the broken lumber at the wheelbarrow. "Maybe so. Looks like this is full."

Linda grabbed the wheelbarrow, pushed it to the pile of firewood, and dumped it. Amanda was glad she didn't press the issue. She was a special lady. Part friend and part mother. As her best friend's mother, she'd done her share over the years of making sure both Amanda and Sarah behaved. She'd always been ready with a word of advice or encouragement when they needed it. Amanda might pretend to brush her insight and wisdom aside, but she knew she would be thinking about their conversation later when she was alone.

They worked hard through the morning to the tune of the chain saw and the men's voices calling to each other. With the sun straight overhead, Elva and Mable joined them. "We've decided someone needs to tell the men it's time to eat."

"Amanda, why don't you do that while we set out the ice chests? Ask if there's a table we can use." Linda turned away with the other two ladies and headed toward the driveway where the vehicles were parked.

Amanda watched them, her hands on her hips, and muttered, "Thanks to you, too. Surely you aren't trying to push me toward Chad just so I can forgive him and forget some long-ago hurt I scarcely remember anyway."

She did an about-face and started toward the house with a shrug. She'd show Linda. She wouldn't remember the night Chad hurt her. With more self-restraint than she knew she had, she forced her mind from the vivid details slithering at the edge of her memory and concentrated on finding her pastor.

The house sat at an angle facing the driveway. She reached the end of the house and stopped short of slamming into Chad as he barreled around the corner.

He caught her by the shoulders and then jerked his hands back as if burned. "I'm sorry." He blinked and shook his head. "Mandy?"

His pet name for her, a name she allowed no one else to use, sounded natural coming from him.

She didn't speak. He stepped back. "I'm sorry, Amanda. I want you to know how thankful I am for your help. You and the group from your church. We've made good progress. We'll have the tree cut up into firewood for the fireplace before the day's over."

"Oh, is it down already?" She stepped to the side and looked past the corner of the house so he couldn't see into her eyes. He might read something that wasn't there. A fog enveloped her brain. Her heart set up a rapid beat.

Beyond a good-sized deck, which covered the closest half of the house, men still worked. Sawdust littered the ground near a huge log that held several large branches. Leaves and broken sticks covered the area, and a large pile of brush leaned against the back fence.

"Yes, it is."

"What is?" Had she asked a question?

"The tree. It's down." His voice dropped to almost a whisper. "You look wonderful, Mandy."

She swung toward him and searched his face without responding. She froze, memorizing every change, every detail she'd only dreamed of for fourteen years. She should be angry with him. She shouldn't stand this close to him or even speak to him. But she found no hurt, no bitterness, and no anger in her heart.

Only a response she didn't want. A response to his presence she couldn't afford. That and curiosity.

Where was his wife? Did he have children?

A thousand questions begged for release, but she asked only one. "We need a table for lunch if that's possible? We've already started getting food out and need a place to put it."

He nodded toward the deck. "There's a table with benches. We can eat out here. I'll pass the word." With that he turned away.

She leaned against the end of the house. As she waited, her heart slowed to a normal beat. A fluffy white cloud drifted past, and she concentrated on it. Like a silly schoolgirl, she let an encounter with her past get way out of proportion. So she once loved Chad. That was long ago. She'd married a wonderful man, and they'd had far too short a life together. Jeffrey. Why did his blond hair darken and his face become Chad's when she tried to bring him to mind? She closed her eyes and gave her head a quick shake to rid it of the troubling thoughts, then pushed away from the house.

She went back to the front yard. Maybe Linda was right. Maybe she shouldn't stay, but she couldn't leave without creating a scene. After today she wouldn't come back.

When she reached the front only Linda waited. Amanda forced a smile. "So where's the food?"

Linda smiled as if she knew something. "They took the ice chests through the house to a deck in back. Let's see what this house looks like. I must admit, I've been curious all morning."

They stepped into the living room. Other than quilts folded on the sofa, the room appeared clean and neat. Amanda assumed Chad slept there the night before. A wide arched doorway opened into the dining room on the back of the house. As they stepped through the arch, they saw where Chad had been trying to clean. Cardboard covered the windows in both the dining room and the kitchen so the rooms were dark and gloomy. She wondered what he wanted them to do, but didn't pursue the thought as the men picked that moment to come inside for more chairs.

After they set out the food, Pastor Mattson prayed and silence fell while everyone helped themselves to sandwiches, potato salad, casseroles, chips, and an assortment of soft drinks kept cold in ice.

With their hunger satisfied, the men began chatting. Amanda paid only enough attention to their conversation to know they were talking about the tree that had been wedged against the house. Rather than listen, she watched Chad join in and laugh with the other men. His smile sent her pulse racing and that annoyed her. She crossed her arms and turned her back toward them. She didn't need the complication. She could ask to be assigned to another location. Or maybe she should start looking for a summer job.

"Seems odd the barn was destroyed and the house almost untouched." Linda's voice penetrated her musings.

She nodded. "Yes, but tornadoes do strange things. I don't imagine any two are alike."

"I heard there were two that night. I wonder if both touched down here."

"Yes, they did." Chad leaned against the railing near them.

Amanda's traitorous heart leapt.

He looked out to where the barn once stood. "The first one damaged the barn. The neighbor said it looked like Steve went out to check the damage. He thought maybe Jess heard about the second tornado on the radio and ran out to tell him. They didn't make it back to the house before it hit."

His voice cracked on the last word and a muscle twitched in his jaw. Amanda brushed at tears pooled in her eyes and swallowed trying to stop any others. She was afraid to speak.

"Kara. Is that your niece?" Linda asked.

He nodded.

"Where is she now?"

Again his jaw clenched. "In foster care. The state swooped in and took her, giving me visiting privileges. That's why it's so important to get this place fixed. When I get it cleaned up and safe, I can bring her home."

"I know you're looking forward to that." Linda smiled. "How old is she?"

"Ten months."

Amanda's breath caught in her throat. Charity was ten months old when she died.

three

Chad watched Amanda while he talked to Linda. He'd always been able to read her expressions, but now he wasn't sure. Pain and grief twisted her features when his sister's name was mentioned. Jessica and Mandy had been close. As close as sisters.

Mandy moved and her auburn hair flashed a brilliant, beautiful red in the sunlight. He used to tease her about her red hair and a temper to match. Her hair was still a shiny auburn. Had her temperament mellowed in the last several years? He didn't know her anymore.

When he mentioned Kara's age, Mandy's face paled and she closed her eyes for a moment. She'd been married. He'd heard her husband died a few years ago in a traffic accident. Had there been a child? If so, where was the child today? He didn't know but wanted to find out. In fact, he wanted to find out all about her. What she'd been doing. Why she was back home. She was a long way from California, so there must be a reason, unless she was here for a visit.

"You ready to go back to work?" John, a likable man in his early forties, joined Chad at the railing. "Looks like we've been given the job of climbing on the roof. The old codgers figure it's too dangerous for them to get more than six feet off the ground."

Chad grinned. "Sure, but has anyone figured out what we'll do up there? We need something to cover the hole. Plastic sheeting would be good, but there probably isn't any available within a hundred miles of here."

John shook his head. "Oh ye of little faith." He pointed to

the men who were just now leaving the table. "Do you see those two old guys with the pastor? One's a retired carpenter. The other's a plumber, almost retired. What one doesn't have, the other does. They brought plastic, just in case. Come on, let's get it up before it rains."

"Good idea." Chad sent one last smile toward Amanda before he followed John and the other men.

Linda called after him, "Hey Chad, we've got a lot of leftovers. Do you care if we put it all in your refrigerator?"

He stopped and shrugged. "That's fine, but I don't have electricity, so if you leave it too long, you may not find any when you return."

Her laughter rang out. "In that case we'll leave the ice, too. And one of the chests. Please do eat it up."

"Don't worry, I will." He waved over his shoulder. "And thanks."

Chad and John worked together well and soon had the sheeting in place. As they nailed the last board over the edge to hold it down, Chad stood and looked over the peak of the roof toward the barn. Amanda had a full wheelbarrow halfway to the firewood pile. If he could get away from the men, he'd take that job from her.

On the ground, he approached the pastor as they walked around the house. "We've got the tree out now, and I'm more grateful than I can express for everything that's been done. Everyone has worked hard all morning. I'm not trying to run you off, but I don't want to wear anyone out, either."

Pastor Mattson smiled and rubbed the back of his neck with his handkerchief. "I was thinking about calling it quits for the day. We don't pull trees out of roofs every day, you know. I'd like to make another workday this coming week if we can. I think all of us except John and Rick are free about anytime. Why don't you name a day, except Wednesday, and we'll make plans to be here?"

"Would Tuesday morning work for you?" Setting a time made Chad feel like a beggar, and he hated that. He needed help, though, for Kara. If he worked alone, she would remain in foster care all summer, and that made begging worthwhile.

"Sounds fine to me." The pastor looked at the other men for confirmation.

By then the women had gathered around, and they all nodded their heads, too. All but Amanda. Chad tried to catch her gaze, but she looked everywhere except at him. His heart sank. She wouldn't be back. She hadn't known he'd be here.

As the group broke up with promises to return, Chad thanked them for their work while he watched Amanda walk to her car. He had to catch her. He might never get the opportunity again. He started toward her when he felt a hand on his arm.

Linda Maddox held him with a stern gaze. "She's been hurt enough."

He watched Amanda open the car door. He looked back at Linda. "I heard her husband died."

She nodded. "Yes, along with her baby. But that isn't all of it."

"Are you talking about us? When we broke up?" Chad didn't understand. It was a long time ago. Yet seeing the girl he'd loved so much had erased the years. More than anything he wanted to tell her how sorry he was. He wanted to apologize because he hadn't been able to back then.

Linda looked away without saying anything for a moment. Finally she turned back to him. "If you talk to her, be careful. Coming here, learning of Jessica's death, seeing you again, it's all opened her emotions, leaving them raw. She's just started getting her life together after losing so much. She doesn't need any more pain."

"I understand about pain and loss." He looked around the

farm and wished for his sister. But she'd never come back. She'd gone home to be with the Lord she loved so much. He had to move on and Amanda needed to, also. Maybe he could help her. If only he could get close enough to talk to her.

He let his gaze settle on Linda. "I won't bother her now, but will you give her a message for me? Will you tell her I need to apologize? I'd like to give her the opportunity to forgive me. Until I have her forgiveness, I doubt I'll ever be able to forgive myself."

Linda searched his face as if looking for the truth. She nodded and turned away. "I'll tell her."

☙

As soon as Linda got in the car and closed the door, Amanda turned the key and the engine started. Chad stood where Linda had left him, watching while they backed out of the driveway.

"Well." Linda let out a rush of air. "I'm glad the Kimbels decided to ride back with the Harrisons."

Amanda watched Chad. "Why did you stop him?"

Linda turned toward Amanda. "To keep him from stopping you."

Amanda glanced at Sarah's mom and laughed. "Sarah always complained you were an overprotective mother. You know, I think she's right."

With a quick wave of her hand, Linda brushed the accusation away. "Oh what does she know? She'll find out soon enough that motherhood isn't all that easy."

Amanda thought of her friend who had been going through the lovely morning sickness stage of pregnancy and giggled. "She's probably getting a good idea of that already. To hear her talk, she's been sleeping in the bathtub to make upchucking easier when she first wakes up. When I told her I only had light nausea with my pregnancy, I thought she was coming through the phone to California so she could choke me."

Linda chuckled. "She was never sick with Trey. Funny how each pregnancy is different."

Amanda nodded. She'd had one baby, and she'd never have another. That thought brought her back to Chad. What had he wanted to talk to her about? True, at the moment she'd wanted to get away from him, but now she wondered. Had he only wanted to thank her for helping? Probably.

"He gave me a message for you." Linda's comment brought a rush of air to Amanda's lungs.

In a tight voice, she asked, "What did he say?"

"He said he wanted to apologize for your past. Then he said something I'm still trying to figure out. He said until you forgive him, he won't be able to forgive himself."

Amanda's grip tightened on the steering wheel. She stopped at the highway, shrugged, and forced a smile. "I'm surprised he realizes he was in the wrong."

"Evidently, he does." Linda looked out the side window as Amanda moved the car forward. "Clear to the right. Oh I'm sorry. I always do that for David."

"That's fine." Amanda kept a smile on her face. "I never object to another pair of eyes."

She pulled out on the highway behind the pastor's car. Rick Harrison's truck followed them.

⁂

The next day Amanda sat in church listening to the report Pastor Mattson gave of their day spent on Chad's farm.

"The Word of God says we are to love our neighbor as ourselves. If our homes had been damaged, our once manicured lawns strewn with trash, broken limbs, and parts of our barn, wouldn't we welcome our neighbor's help? Removing a large tree from the roof of a house is impossible for one man alone. Yesterday, with the expertise of our men, and by working together, we turned that monumental task into a congenial time of hard work mixed with fellowship. The women also did a tremendous job of cleaning up the yard."

He seemed to look right at her when he said, "We've agreed to return Tuesday. There's much work to be done before Mr. Randall can bring his orphaned niece home. The little girl, less than a year old, is in foster care now, and he desperately wants her with him. He feels she needs to be with family, and I sensed in talking to him, he needs her just as much, as she's all the family he has left."

All the family he has left. The words rang in Amanda's ears until she could hear nothing else. Chad had no family? No wife? No children? But he was married. What happened in his life that she knew nothing about? Her parents had never told her anything other than a passing mention that Chad and Jessica's mother passed away. That was a couple of years ago. She searched her memory and could think of no other mention of Chad. Did her mom know anything else?

She stole a peek at her mother who seemed to be listening with nothing other than interest in her expression. What about Linda? Amanda turned slightly to look across the church where Linda and David Maddox sat. Linda caught her gaze and smiled before turning her attention back to the pastor.

All the family he has left. The congregation stood as the liturgist read the scripture selection taken from Luke 10. Amanda followed in her Bible while he read the story of the Good Samaritan. She couldn't stay focused on Pastor Mattson's sermon, as his earlier statement wouldn't leave her alone. If Chad had no family other than his niece. . . No, she wouldn't entertain such thoughts. She'd almost married Chad once, but he'd proved his love was fleeting. He might be attracted to her. She couldn't deny her attraction to him, but that's all it was. Some strange chemical reaction that had already been and would again be the cause of disaster if she allowed it to. And she wouldn't. Her life was starting to come together after five years of uncertainty. She had to forget Chad, and the best way was to stay away from him.

At the end of the service, Amanda followed her parents to the door where the pastor stood shaking hands. He held hers with both of his and gave her a wide smile. "Amanda, I want you to know how thankful we are to have you back here with us."

"Thank you, Pastor."

He released her hand. "I don't think I've ever worked as hard as I did yesterday, but I wouldn't have missed it. I know you understand, and I imagine you're looking forward to Tuesday as much as I am."

"Yes." Not because she'd be on Chad's farm. She couldn't do that, but she did look forward to each new day.

He nodded as if she'd agreed. "It'll be worth it all to get that baby back with her uncle, won't it? She's lost her mom and dad. Just doesn't seem right for her to be kept from a loving uncle, too."

Each sentence the pastor uttered became a tiny prod, poking and urging her to admit she cared about Chad, that she'd be there Tuesday to help. Her heart went out to the baby she'd never met. What if her baby had lived and she'd died along with Jeff? She'd have wanted Karen or Brad to take her and raise her as their own. A baby belonged with family who would love and want her as much as Chad seemed to. Even single, Chad would be a good father to his niece. Amanda believed that.

☙

After a noisy dinner with her brother's family in attendance, Amanda washed the dishes. Brad came into the kitchen for another slice of their mother's chocolate cake. He took a plate and fork from the dish drainer.

"Hey, I just washed that." She was wasting her breath but tried anyway.

He grinned and cut a big slice of cake. "Good, you'll know how to do it again when I'm done. They say practice makes perfect."

"I'm not going to stand here and wash dishes all afternoon so you can stuff your face." She grabbed another plate and fork and cut her own slice. "Instead, I'll join you. How come your two hooligans aren't in here grabbing more cake, too?"

"Oh, Dad's got them looking through his stamp collection. They're about as quiet as I've ever seen them, so I took advantage of it." He grinned. "Mom and Esther went upstairs to look at some fabric for a quilt or something, so they can't say anything if I eat up the cake."

Amanda laughed. "You won't eat it all. Together we won't even eat it all. It's too rich. When Mom makes chocolate cake, she makes it really chocolate."

"Yeah. So how's life treating you now?" Brad's question caught her by surprise.

"Fine. I'm looking forward to my first teaching job." She sighed. "I do need a summer job, though. I'd like to get a place of my own. Living here makes me feel seventeen again."

He grinned. "That doesn't sound so bad."

She smiled until he said, "I heard you've been helping clean up Chad Randall's place after those tornadoes."

"I went yesterday, but I didn't know who owned the farm until I was already there."

A gleam she couldn't decipher entered his eyes. "So, I heard he's single now. You are, too."

She stuck her fork in her half-eaten cake and glared at her brother. "That's exactly right, and I plan to stay that way. I'm not sure what you're getting at, but I have no plans of going within ten miles of Chad Randall again if I can help it. So take your matchmaking someplace else."

As if he hadn't heard her outburst, he asked, "Did you even stop to consider that he might've been innocent all those years ago?"

"Innocent? Ha!" The anger and hurt rushed through her as if she'd just that moment found Chad and Susan together. "I saw him and—oh forget it." She stood and set her plate to the side. "There's no point in discussing this. It's past and needs to stay there right along with Chad Randall. I won't be helping Tuesday. That's all there is to it."

Before her brother could say something else she didn't want to hear, she walked from the room and ran upstairs. Voices came from her mother's sewing room. She slipped past the open door and breathed easier when neither her mother nor her sister-in-law called out to her. They both loved to sew and probably had their heads together over a stack of material. Tiptoeing the rest of the way, she went into her room and closed the door.

She sprawled across her bed facedown and rested her head on her bent arm. The temper she'd displayed toward her brother had already ebbed away. She hadn't been angry with Brad. Her anger was caused by her conflicting emotions. Feelings stirred by seeing Chad after so many years.

He looked good. His dark hair was still thick and wavy. His face as strong and handsome as ever, only the added creases in the corners of his eyes when he smiled made him even more appealing. She sighed. He'd been so alive and wonderful when he spoke to her and smiled as if she meant something to him. But she didn't. Oh, maybe a little, but not enough. Never enough.

She jumped from the bed and pulled her cell phone from her purse then plopped back down and found her sister's name in contacts. While the phone rang, she lay back and stared at the ceiling.

"Hello?"

"Karen, are you coming to Mom and Dad's this evening?"

"Of course. I haven't seen my little sister since she moved home. How's that going, by the way?"

Amanda suppressed a sigh. "Fine, but I'd like to get my own place ASAP. That isn't why I called, though. I need to return a rental car. If you're coming here anyway, could you meet me at the Springfield airport and let me ride back home with you?"

"Sure, that's not a problem. What time?"

After they'd made arrangements, Amanda grabbed her purse and went downstairs to tell her parents what she was doing. Brad followed her to the car and held the door while she got in. "Hey, I'm sorry for what I said in the kitchen."

"That's all right." She smiled, her anger forgotten. "I know you mean well."

He grinned. "Actually, that's true. I do. So I guess you'll understand when I say I always liked Chad. I think he got set up. Did you know he married Susan?"

"What?" Amanda scarcely remembered to close her mouth. "And that proves his innocence? Come on, Brad, what are you thinking?"

"In a nutshell? She set him up. The whole thing. She staged that display for your benefit to break you and Chad up so she could get her claws into him."

"She was my college roommate. She would have been one of my bridesmaids." Amanda shook her head. "That night, she broke away from him and ran to me. She was crying. She thanked me for stopping him. We went back to the dorm and I never spoke to him again—or her—after that night."

A harsh laugh escaped Brad. "She thanked you? She knew you. She counted on your quick temper. Just think about it, okay? You're young. You don't want to carry this bitterness for the rest of your life no matter how long that may be. Pray for Chad and his little niece."

He closed her door without waiting for her promise, but she knew she'd be praying for Chad, for Kara, and for herself. What happened to Susan? Brad said Chad married her. How did he know? Why hadn't he ever told her? She'd already pulled from the driveway and started down the street before the implication of what he'd said sank in. Chad and Susan married? Living together, having children together. Pain such as she hadn't experienced since that night hit her, and she pulled to the side of the street to will it away. She couldn't still hurt this much because of Chad. He meant nothing to her anymore.

After several moments, she put the gearshift back into drive, followed the street west to Interstate 55, and headed toward Springfield. At the airport she returned the car and called Karen who agreed to meet her at the front doors. When she saw Karen's blue compact car, she ran out and climbed in the front seat.

"Where's Wayne? And the kids?"

Karen pulled away from the curb and followed the drive around to the exit. "I wanted some special sister time, so they stayed home. We'll pick them up before we head south."

"Okay, sounds great."

"So, tell me about this job teaching. When does school start? Are you excited? I'm so proud of you. I can't believe how much you've accomplished in the last few years."

"Since the accident."

Karen nodded. "Yeah, since then. You went through a lot. Maybe now you'll find someone special and replace the family you lost."

Tears sprang to Amanda's eyes at her sister's careless words. "You can't replace people, Karen. No one will ever take the place of those I lost."

"Oh, I'm sorry." Karen took her hand from the steering wheel and touched Amanda's arm. "I didn't mean it that way.

I was thinking of Job in the Bible. Remember how he lost his children along with almost everything he owned? God restored all that he'd lost. That included his kids. His family. I only meant maybe God has someone for you. You're still young."

Amanda looked out the side window and brushed at her eyes. "You know I can't have children. Men want whole women, not damaged goods."

"Giving birth is not what makes a woman whole, Amanda." Karen's voice held a touch of annoyance. "You know that, and I don't know how we got on this treadmill, anyway. You believe whatever you want to, because far be it from me to talk sense into you."

Amanda laughed. "Does a little bit of temper run in our family?"

Karen grinned and fluffed her auburn hair, which held even more red than Amanda's. "Wayne says this red highlighting has seeped right down into my brain cells and sets me off now and then. I told him I'd wash it out if I could, but God gave it to me, so He must've wanted me with a little spice."

"Yeah, I blew up at Brad this afternoon when he stuck his nose in my business."

"Oh my, you're gettin' hit from all sides, aren't you?" Karen's green eyes sparkled as she smiled. "Come on, tell me about it."

"No." Amanda frowned. "He just thinks I should help out with the tornado victims."

"So, he's right. Why wouldn't you help out? You've got the summer free, don't you? Besides, it's a great way to get out of the house."

"I did help. One day." Amanda turned back to the window.

Karen drove in silence for too short a time. "Okay, I can't figure it out. If you don't tell me why you won't go back, I'll ask Brad." She picked up her cell phone and flipped it open.

Amanda swung around. "Don't you dare."

"Then tell." She closed the phone and put it back on the seat beside her.

"This isn't fair." Amanda folded her arms, but she'd tell. What difference did it make? Karen knew all her secrets, anyway.

"It's what you get for being the baby. Now go on. Spill."

Amanda sighed. "Chad Randall."

"What?"

"Chad's sister and her husband died in the tornadoes, leaving their ten-month-old daughter. Chad's trying to get the farm cleaned up enough to bring her home. She's in foster care right now."

"Oh that poor baby." Karen pulled off the road into a vacant parking lot and stopped the car. She turned to look at her sister. "Are you going to let an old hurt keep you from helping that child? This isn't like you, Amanda. Whatever happened between you and Chad was a long time ago. You can't still be carrying a flame for him, can you?"

"Of course not." Amanda's eyes widened at the thought of everyone thinking exactly that if she refused to go back. "Besides, I am going back to help. Why wouldn't I?"

She refused to acknowledge Karen's smug smile as she started the car and drove back onto the road.

four

"This doesn't look so bad." Amanda stood in the middle of the dining room floor at the farm and looked around.

Linda set a bucket of supplies on the floor. She turned slowly, taking in the room. "True, but let's have a look-see. These windows were broken. I'll bet we find glass pieces in unexpected places, so be careful."

"You ladies doing okay?" Chad walked across the room and ripped the cardboard off the window. Sunlight streamed through the opening. "Now maybe you can see what this place really looks like. I picked up the mess and swept up the worst of it, but there's dirt and grime that blew in and broken glass. Please, don't get cut."

Amanda met his gaze. Had he singled her out in his concern? More likely he'd been looking her way by chance. She broke the connection first. She could do this. She could work near him and not let her imagination run wild. Such as thinking Chad cared for her.

Chad went into the kitchen and uncovered the windows there, too. As light flooded the rooms, Amanda saw the film of dust covering every surface. A sparkle revealed a sliver of glass wedged at the corner of the refrigerator on the floor. She went into the utility room for the broom.

"Sorry we're late." Elva and Mable came in as Amanda started back toward the kitchen. "What do you want us to do?"

Amanda stopped short as Chad came through the door and almost collided with her. He grinned but didn't step away, leaving her the choice of backing up or staying where she was. She decided backing up would be like blurting out to him and everyone else that Chad sent her blood pressure into overdrive. She stayed, took deep, slow breaths, and turned to face the two women.

Before she could remember what they'd asked, Chad spoke, "I appreciate you ladies pitching in to help. The house has to be clean and safe before I can bring Kara here, and I don't have time to work on it with everything outside that needs attention, too. That and the legal red tape are keeping me pretty busy."

"We're glad to help." Elva spoke up. "You tell us what needs doing and go about your business. We'll get it done. We want that little girl with you where she belongs."

"Thanks." He stepped around Amanda without so much as a look. "The two bedrooms on the back of the house were hit pretty hard. Especially Kara's room."

Elva and Mable followed Chad down the hall toward the back while Amanda turned to the kitchen. Linda ran water in the sink and started cleaning.

"I saw some glass Chad missed." Amanda took the broom. "I thought I'd sweep these two rooms first. I suppose even the walls and woodwork need to be wiped down."

Linda leaned forward and swiped her finger down the window casing. She stuck her finger out for Amanda to see. "Wouldn't hurt. The refrigerator needs to be cleaned, too. Power's been off a week. Wonder when that'll come back on."

"I don't know. I noticed an oil lamp and some candles in the living room. Chad's been indoor camping."

"It isn't so bad."

Amanda twirled around and almost dropped her broom at the sound of his voice entirely too close behind her.

"Sorry." He jumped back, his hands out. "I didn't mean to startle you."

His grin said otherwise. He reached past her, opened a drawer, and pulled out a hammer.

"You have tools in the kitchen?" Amanda couldn't resist asking.

"Sure, it's called a tool drawer." His quick wink sent her heart pounding.

He turned and walked out through the dining room to the deck. She held her hand over her heart to slow its beating, glad Linda stood behind her at the sink and couldn't see. No sense in letting everyone witness her infuriating responses to Chad.

"Amanda." Linda's voice was soft but firm. "Maybe this isn't a good idea."

"What?" She turned and looked at Linda with wide, innocent eyes. At least she hoped she looked innocent. "Do you want me to work on the counters first?"

"That isn't what I mean, and you know it. Go ahead and sweep, but tell me something. Do you have feelings for Chad?"

Amanda glanced toward the door when she heard pounding against the side of the house. Chad using his hammer, no doubt. "How could I have feelings for anyone? I've been so busy the last few years working and finishing school, I haven't had time for romance. I still don't."

Linda smirked. "Good evasion. So the answer's yes. What are you going to do about it?"

"Nothing." Amanda resumed sweeping. She pushed her pile of dirt toward the dining room, catching the sliver of glass as she went. "My feelings don't matter, anyway. Chad doesn't care about me. He proved that a long time ago."

"I don't know what happened, and you don't need to tell me." Linda kept her voice soft. "But there's one thing I do know. Unforgiveness hurts the person who refuses to forgive. And another thing. There's always two sides to any disagreement. I know you, Amanda. You have a quick temper, but you'd rather walk away than fight for your rights."

"What is this? Pick on Amanda week?" She swept her dirt into a pile and held the dustpan in place.

Linda wiped out the sink and started on the counters before responding. "Just think about what I've said, okay?"

Amanda moved into the dining room, sweeping and muttering as she went. "Sure, you and Brad and Karen, not to mention Mom and Dad. I'm glad everyone else knows what I should do."

Linda's chuckle followed her.

Amanda had swept the dining room when she heard scraping sounds and pounding overhead. She took a bucket of water and some rags and began cleaning every washable surface. She used wood polish she found in the pantry and dusted the table, chairs, and sideboard. From the quality of the house and furniture, Jessica and Steve had done well for themselves. Maybe they both worked. She had to work while Jeff was in college, which is why she didn't go back to school after they married.

By noon the dining room and kitchen passed Linda's exacting standards. Amanda had even found time to clean the bathroom, although it didn't appear to have suffered any damage and didn't need more than a quick going over.

Elva and Mable brought a basket of laundry from the back and left it in the utility room. Mable shook her head. "The baby's room was a mess. I don't know how the little thing survived."

"The baby bed is in the corner near the outside wall. The window broke, but we couldn't find any pieces in the bed. No blood, either, so she wasn't cut. Surely God kept His hand upon her." Elva's lips pursed as she sighed. "She must've been so frightened. I can't imagine what that baby suffered in here all alone with so many loud noises going on."

While the older women talked, Amanda's heart grew heavy with compassion for the baby. Charity would have screamed in fear. Had Kara screamed and no one heard her? Had she cried herself to sleep when no one came? Even without seeing the baby, Amanda longed to hold her close and comfort her. *Lord, please be with little Kara. Help Chad make a good home for her. Bring everything together here so they can be a family.*

Elva stuck her head out the patio doors and called to the men outside, "Are you at a place where you can stop for lunch? We've got sandwiches. It isn't much, but it'll knock the hunger away."

"You bet," Ron's deep voice answered.

Amanda heard him yell to the other men. The scraping sounds overhead intensified until all grew quiet and the three men showed up on the deck. John and Rick had been unable to return.

Chad came in for the ice chest. He grinned at Amanda. "Drinks are on me today. I filled the chest you left Saturday with ice and soda."

They set the sandwiches and cans of soda on the dining room table. They gathered inside for prayer then took their filled plates outside. Amanda watched Chad. He seemed so relaxed. His smile came easily, but it always had. She'd loved that about him. He hadn't joked about life, but he'd faced its challenges with optimism.

Now he moved and stood with tension. Did anyone else notice? She saw pain deep in his blue eyes. He hurt more than he let on. Did he have anyone to talk to? He'd married Susan, but he was single now. What did that mean?

When she'd lost Jeff and Charity, she'd had her in-laws. She couldn't count the times she and Janice had cried together. Who did Chad have to cry with? Did he have the Lord to help him?

Amanda finished her sandwich and stood while the others visited. She stepped off the deck and walked around the house, looking at the damage. Sawdust and wood chips littered the yard. The fallen tree was now a large pile of short logs. Amazingly, the wall where the tree had fallen didn't appear to be damaged at all. Makeshift screens had been tacked over the broken bedroom window.

After she rounded the corner of the house, a twig popped behind her. She knew before she turned.

"Chad." She forced a smile. "I hadn't seen this part of the house yet. Is this where most of the damage is?"

He nodded. "Kara's bedroom. Amazing, isn't it? That she's alive, I mean. The tree could've crushed her. The broken glass could've cut her, or she could've been sucked out the window. She didn't get a scratch and doesn't seem to be affected by it at all, except she wants her mother."

"God had His hand on her."

He gave a short, bitter laugh. "Maybe, but why'd He take Jessica?"

"I don't know." She'd asked the same question so many times and still didn't have the answers. Why did God take one and leave another? Why had she been left?

She stopped and faced Chad. "Maybe God didn't take Jessica and Steve. Maybe He only welcomed them home."

Chad stared into her eyes for a long moment as if trying to understand. Finally, he looked away and shrugged. "I guess it doesn't matter. They're gone and Kara's still here. I've got to make a home for her and she hates me."

"What?" That was the last thing she expected to hear him say. "How could she hate you? She's a baby."

He folded his arms and leaned back against the house. "Yes, a baby that screams when I get close to her."

"When did you see her last?"

"Sunday. I go this coming Sunday afternoon." He captured her gaze. "Will you go with me? Please, Amanda. I wouldn't ask, but I really don't think I can go through that again. Not alone. Please?"

She stared at the ground trying to decide what to say. What to do. He had no idea how much she wanted to hold his niece close and love her. She was Jessica's baby and she'd loved Jessica like a sister. She would love her baby, too. She knew she would. How could she, though? This was Chad. The man who had betrayed her with her friend. He was engaged to her, but he married Susan. Why had Susan married him if he'd done what she said? She wanted answers, but she didn't want to ask the questions.

She looked up. "I don't know—"

"Don't answer now," he interrupted. "This is only Tuesday. Why don't you think about it? Pray about it if you want. I'm not trying to crowd you, Amanda. I'm only asking for help, and surely you know I wouldn't if I didn't need it. May I call you Friday evening? That'll give you time to decide if you can trust me."

"I don't. . ." Her voice trailed off because she couldn't honestly say she trusted him.

He grinned at her. "I'm not as bad as you think. Can't we be friends? Maybe we can talk sometime. Get caught up on each other's lives. I've got about a thousand questions for you. I figure you might think up a couple to ask me."

Amanda sighed. "All right. I'll give you my cell number." If he had a thousand questions, she had a couple all right. A couple of thousand.

What would it hurt to have her curiosity satisfied?

☙

Amanda spent Wednesday and Thursday looking for work. Summer jobs weren't as easy to find as she'd expected. Seemed the high school and college kids had already snatched them up. She put in several applications, even making the rounds of the fast-food restaurants with little encouragement. After handing one more application to a prospective employer, she drove back to her folks' house in her mother's car. She had enough money from the sale of her car and furniture in California to buy her own transportation, but she'd hoped to have some income before she did.

Relying on her parents had been one of the reasons she hadn't wanted to move to Litchfield. Mom didn't seem to mind having Dad chauffeur her to and from work, but Amanda minded a lot. She needed a job soon. One that wouldn't interfere with her school duties. She had orientation workshops later in the summer to attend and there would be lesson plans to ready for teaching. She'd need some time to prepare her classroom and materials. Which meant she'd probably only have a couple of months to work before preparing to teach. Sometimes just thinking about it both overwhelmed and excited her. She could scarcely wait until that first day of school.

She pulled down the street to her house when her cell phone played the default melody. Curious, she turned it on and answered.

"Amanda?" Chad's voice set her pulse racing. He said he'd call Friday evening, not Thursday afternoon.

"Yes." She wouldn't let him know she recognized his voice.

"It's Chad. You said I could call."

"I expected you to call tomorrow." She pulled into the drive at the house and stopped. "Am I wrong, or isn't this Thursday?"

He chuckled. "I got lonely."

"So you called my number?"

"Best number in my phone. Even has a picture."

"You took a picture of me? In grungy work clothes with dirt all over my face and, I might add, without my permission or knowledge." She couldn't stop the pleased smile from spreading, although she'd never let him know.

"Oops, am I in trouble?" He didn't sound the least bit worried. She heard the smile in his voice. "It's a really nice picture and there isn't any dirt that I can see. Just a beautiful woman."

Now she did smile. "You would use flattery to get out of trouble?"

"I don't know, I might, but I'm not." His voice dropped. "I always thought you were the prettiest girl I'd ever seen."

He couldn't mean that, not after what he'd done. His words, meant to flatter, had the opposite effect, dousing Amanda with reality. If he meant what he said, why'd he take second best? Why had he married Susan? She didn't want to think about it, so she said, "Did you call to set up a time and place Sunday?"

"Then you'll go with me?" The lilt in his voice held a bit of relief as well.

"If you remember, Jessica and I were very close at one time. I'm going for her. I don't know that I'll be any help, but I'm willing to meet you at the foster home and see what happens." She opened the car door and stepped out. Her dad's truck wasn't in the drive, so that meant no one would be at home. Maybe she could start supper so Mom wouldn't have to.

"Why don't you stop at the farm? We can go from here so I don't have to give you directions."

His idea had merit. If she followed him from the farm, she still wouldn't be riding with him, sitting beside him, trying to think of something to say. She unlocked the kitchen door and went into the house. She set her purse on the table and opened the refrigerator. "Okay, I guess that will work."

"Great, can you be here around two o'clock?"

"Sure." She closed the refrigerator and opened the freezer. She'd thaw a pound of hamburger. She could make spaghetti or something. She turned on the cold water and plugged the sink.

"Now that's settled, how about a question–answer session?

Or are you too busy? Sounds like you're running water."

She laughed. "I'm in the kitchen. Mom isn't home from work yet, so I thought I'd thaw some hamburger to get a head start on supper. I'm about done for now."

"Okay, do you want to ask first or shall I?"

Amanda dropped the package of hamburger in the water and headed toward the living room, totally intrigued with the idea of finding answers to questions that had badgered her for fourteen years. She'd gone to meet Susan that night to talk over a personal problem her friend had. They'd chosen a quiet city park off campus for the privacy it afforded. Susan was already there, but Amanda hadn't known that until she rounded the hedge sheltering that corner of the park. Susan was with someone. Chad. Wrapped in his arms. Oh yes, the whys of that night would probably take up half of her questions. But she couldn't ask them. Not over the phone.

She sat in her dad's recliner and lifted the footrest. "You go first. I'll save my questions until later."

"All right if you're sure, I'd like to know what your intentions are. Are you in the area for a visit or is this something more permanent?" Chad's question was followed by a loud thump.

"What was that?"

He chuckled. "Already you're asking questions and you haven't even answered mine. I just found a box in Kara's room that might have water damage. Looks like clothes in here. Maybe some Jessica had stored away. Figured I'd better check for mold. Now, how about you answer me?"

"I moved back. I'm looking for a summer job that's flexible enough to let me prepare for school."

"School?"

"Yes, teaching kindergarten. This will be my first year."

"Is that right?" He sounded either pleased or amused. Amanda couldn't tell which.

"I'm very excited, although I'm well aware of the attention

to detail that's required. I made up a checklist of things to do before the first day of school, and it's three pages long." She laughed. "I've already started preparing some of the materials I'll be using. It's kind of fun."

"I've about forgotten my first year, but I'm sure I was excited. Fun? I'm not so sure." He chuckled. "You'll settle in and it'll get easier with each year. At least that's what they keep telling me."

"So, you did go into teaching?"

"That was the plan, wasn't it?" His voice roughened around the words that brought a flood of memories to her mind.

Her sophomore year of high school, she walked into the classroom where the FTA club, Future Teachers of America, met. That was the first time she'd noticed Chad. His dark good looks and ready smile drew her like a magnet. She slipped into the empty chair in front of him and said, "Hi."

He was a senior, in the same class with her brother, when they started dating. Two years later, by the end of her senior year, they were talking marriage. He would teach high school history while she taught elementary. During their summer vacations, they'd travel.

She attended the state university in Springfield along with him through her first two years. Just before his graduation, they became officially engaged and would have been married that summer, if she hadn't found him with Susan.

"Amanda?" His voice in her ear and the crunch of tires on the driveway outside brought her back to the present. "I'm sorry if I said something I shouldn't have."

"No of course not." She let the footrest down and stood. "Listen, my folks just got here, so I'd better go. I'll meet you Sunday at the farm. Bye, Chad."

She hung up before he could stop her. She'd do this one last good deed for Jessica's little girl, and then she was finished. No more Chad, no more farm, no Kara. She didn't need any of them.

five

Sunday morning Amanda was surprised to see Chad at church. When he stood and thanked the people for helping him, she had to brush away a tear. "I can't express the feeling I have when I think of the way you pitched in and helped a stranger in need. I couldn't have done what you did. Thank you isn't enough."

After church Chad stopped Amanda. "I'll see you this afternoon, right?"

His eyes held uncertainty and touched her heart. She nodded. "Yes, you did say around two, didn't you?"

"Yes, and thanks, Mandy. I'll be watching for you." He smiled and walked away.

Two hours later, Amanda stopped behind a black extended cab truck. She hadn't paid special attention to Chad's truck before today, but the shiny exterior and clean, empty bed with the black, unmarred liner, told her he used it for highway and city driving. Dad's truck had dings and scrapes from hauling anything from furniture to firewood and brush.

Chad stepped out the front door before she reached the porch. His smile came easy, but she recognized the tension in his posture and around his eyes.

"Hey, you ready to go?" He walked with her toward his truck.

"Sure, I'll pull out first, and you can lead the way." She started toward her car, but he stopped her.

"Mandy."

She turned slowly back to him. "Maybe you shouldn't call me that."

His eyes darkened. "Maybe not, but I'd like to. Are you afraid of me?"

She gave a quick laugh. "Afraid? Of what? Of course not. I've never known you to be a violent person."

"You know I'm not talking physical." He held her gaze. "We need to talk. Not today and not over the phone. But soon. You and I have unfinished business. There are things I've never understood that I'd like to. Things I hope you can explain."

Her head nodded, although she scarcely realized it. She wanted answers, too. She wanted him to tell her so many things. Over the years she fooled herself into believing she didn't care. She avoided any mention of Chad or Susan. She left school, and refusing to listen to anyone, had gone as far as she could from Illinois. But not from the comfort of her faith. She met Jeffrey at church. And used him as an escape from her pain.

"Move your car out of the way and get in the truck with me. There's no sense in taking two vehicles." He stood and waited while she obeyed.

If he hadn't been right, she might've held out, because truthfully, she was afraid of him. She hadn't forgotten him any more than her heart had. Seeing him again brought them together in a way that seemed almost as if they'd never parted on one level, but had suffered a terrible separation on another. One that needed to be worked through before they could get on with their separate lives.

She sat in the bucket seat and leaned her head back on the headrest. Like Chad, his truck was neat and clean. He'd always kept his vehicles in good condition. He obviously hadn't changed in that respect. She lifted her head and slanted a look toward him. "So, what do you plan to do with the farm once it's back in shape? Will you live here?"

He shrugged. "I live in Rockford, so the place won't do

Kara or me any good."

"Are you getting it ready to sell?"

"Yeah. That doesn't bother you, does it?" Chad looked at her. "I mean helping out when I'm going to sell the place."

"No, of course not." Amanda shook her head, but really she didn't know how she felt about the farm belonging to someone else. It wasn't her business, but somehow the thought of someone else taking over Jessica's home did bother her.

"I might keep it, except in time Kara won't remember this place."

"You're taking her with you?" The question was out before she could stop it. Of course he'd take his niece with him. Was Susan still in the picture? Even if they weren't still married, what would happen when he brought a baby home? Would that make a difference in their relationship?

He frowned. "Of course, I'm taking her. She's all I've got now."

They entered the city limits and neither spoke for a few minutes as they drove through the cleanup still in progress and turned south. On the south edge of town, Chad stopped in front of a rambling old Victorian house. Amanda loved old houses, and this one was charming with its wraparound front porch and curlicue trim on all the corners. A cement walk led them across the wide lawn to the front steps. She'd never thought of what a foster home should look like, but if there was a pattern, this should be it. If only the people were as welcoming and warm as their house.

Chad turned what looked like a large flat turnkey, and they heard the *brrring*ing sound outside.

"Oh how wonderful." Amanda laughed. "I didn't know those old door ringers were still in existence."

"They probably aren't outside a museum." Chad grinned. "Except for this one."

"Is the foster mother as old as the house?" Amanda widened her eyes.

Chad chuckled. "Thankfully, no."

At that moment the door opened and a teenage girl, her dark brown hair in a ponytail, motioned them in. "Hi, Mom says come to the family room. That's where Babycakes is."

"Babycakes?" Amanda had to ask.

The girl grinned. "That's my name for Kara. She's got these cute, fat little cheeks, so I call her Babycakes. Don't ask why, 'cause I don't know."

She spoke over her shoulder as she led them through two large rooms before they reached the family room. "I'm Jana, by the way."

"Glad to meet you, Jana. I'm Amanda, and I love your house."

Jana shrugged. "Thanks, it's pretty, I guess, but that's just the face it shows the world. Truthfully, it's just a big, old drafty barn. We love it, though."

"There you are." An older version of Jana sat on the sofa with the baby and a book. She stood and walked toward them and smiled at Amanda. "Hi, I'm Kathy Warner."

"I'm Amanda Wilson, a friend of Chad's."

Amanda sensed Chad stiffen as Kathy approached. Jessica's little girl was adorable, just as she knew she would be. The fat, little cheeks Jana had mentioned looked kissable. Amanda could scarcely wait to hold her, but she stepped back to allow Chad access.

"Look here, sweetie, Uncle Chad has come to see you." The foster mother shifted Kara so she faced her uncle.

For long moments, Chad watched the baby as if she might bite him if he moved too quickly. Finally he held his hands out. She shrank back against the woman, curling her shoulder up against her chin while her large, blue eyes stared back at him.

"Let's sit together on the floor with some toys," Kathy suggested. She moved close to a corner where a pile of baby toys waited.

Amanda nudged Chad, so together they followed and sat with legs crossed on the floor. Kathy put Kara in the middle of the semicircle they made and motioned toward the toys. "Why don't you hand her something? See if you can get her to play with you."

Chad looked at Amanda with pain in his eyes, and she almost buckled. Kara was his niece. He had to connect with her if he expected to take her home. She watched him pick up a small, soft ball and hand it to Kara. His eyes widened when she took it and some of the starch dissolved from his posture. Amanda was so proud when he got Kara to throw the ball to him. At least she opened her hands and it rolled his direction. She squealed when he didn't toss it back immediately. Amanda laughed and he relaxed a little more.

Kathy eased back and soon sat in the chair a few feet away watching with a soft smile on her lips.

Amanda itched to hold the little one who brought memories of Jessica to mind. She didn't know whether to release the tears pressing against her eyes or let loose the laughter that bubbled at every cute expression that brought back memories of her own baby. She knew she'd lost her heart from the moment she saw Jessica's daughter. Seeing her squeal in play or watch Chad with large wary eyes filled Amanda's heart with love such as she knew wasn't healthy. She would pay for this visit later with the unfulfilled pain of longing for a child of her own. Of longing for Charity. Missing the sweet times.

Kara soon tired of their game. She leaned forward and caught herself on her hands. Before either of them could react, she was crawling toward Kathy's rocker. Amanda wouldn't let her get away. She reached past Chad and caught the baby. Speaking softly to her, she picked her up.

"Hey, where do you think you're going?" She smiled at the little girl and stood with her, walking away from Kathy. She motioned for Chad to follow her.

Kara leaned back in Amanda's arms and studied her with a serious expression. Amanda kept talking to her and smiling while she walked around the room. "You are such a pretty girl. You look so much like your mommy did. Her eyes were exactly that same pretty shade of blue."

She shifted her to sit on her arm. "Like Uncle Chad has. Have you seen his pretty blue eyes lately?"

Amanda glanced at Chad who stood in the center of the room watching her. The hint of a smile touched his lips in answer to hers. Kara patted Amanda's face as if demanding full attention. Amanda laughed. Charity used to do the same thing. It would be too easy to pretend she held Charity. She couldn't do that to herself or to Kara.

"Let's go see Uncle Chad's pretty eyes."

"Pretty?" His eyebrows rose in challenge while his lips twitched as if he wanted to smile but wouldn't let himself.

"Oops, I mean handsome. Men are so easily offended." As she talked and drew closer to Chad, Kara's watchful expression turned to trust.

Kathy stood and motioned to herself and then toward the door. Amanda nodded. She was going to leave them alone. Maybe with her gone, Chad would have a chance to become friends with Kara. She hoped so.

Kara found a button on Amanda's shirt and concentrated on trying to pick it up between her thumb and finger. Amanda stood so close to Chad, she could sense his uncertainty and tension.

"Chad, relax." She gave him a smile. "She's a baby. She reacts to the way you feel. Even I can feel your fear of her. Just love her. That's all she needs right now."

"I do love her." Chad ground the words out through his teeth. "Why wouldn't I? She's part of Jessica."

"Then take her. Hold her and tell her so she believes you." Amanda set Kara in Chad's reluctant arms but stayed close for her to continue playing with her button. Of course that meant she had to practically lean against Chad. In reality, she could have run a hand between them without touching, but she still felt his warmth. She felt his tension, too, and that troubled her.

"Look, Kara." Amanda tapped against a button on Chad's shirt. "Uncle Chad has buttons, too." She took the button between finger and thumb and held it out for Kara to see.

Kara turned to the new attraction, letting Amanda's button go. Chad's was smaller and she couldn't get her fingers to latch on. She looked up at Chad as if to ask for help and stared at the unexpected face.

Chad tried to smile. Amanda had to give him credit for that. Before he could muster up a full-fledged smile, though, Kara's little face scrunched and her mouth opened to let out a cry that tore through Amanda's heart. Pudgy little hands reached for Amanda just before she lunged, almost falling from Chad's grasp.

They caught her at the same time and Chad let go. Amanda held her close and patted her back, softly talking to her. "You're fine. There's nothing to be frightened of. Uncle Chad loves you, Kara. He wants to hold you and let you be his little girl. He's just a little afraid right now, so you'll have to help."

As she talked, Chad sank into the nearest chair, his face hidden by his hands. Amanda's heart carried the burden of his pain. She'd loved him once. She'd trusted him and he'd betrayed her. She thought he'd killed any chance of her ever loving him again, but now she didn't know. Something had flared to life for just a moment. Maybe if she covered the spark with the painful memories of their breakup, it wouldn't come back to life to hurt her again.

Kathy came back after that and talked Chad into trying again to play with Kara along with all of them. Jana and her younger sister, Teri, joined them and soon had Kara laughing and squealing. Amanda watched Chad and knew his pain was real. His niece had rejected him for strangers and he didn't know what to do about it. Soon he would have to take her home. How would they get along then?

By the time their visit ended, Amanda had lost her heart to Kara. She held the baby for Chad to kiss bye, then she squeezed her close, loving the feel of her tiny body in her arms. Charity had not seemed so close, yet so far away, since she died. She kissed Kara's cheek and a tear slid from her eye. She couldn't let this little girl into her heart only to be hurt again. She just couldn't.

She handed her to Kathy and forced a smile as she wiped her tears away. She couldn't explain why she was crying so she only said, "She's so sweet."

"Yes, she is." Kathy turned Kara away when she reached for Amanda, babbling in her own baby language. Kathy looked at Chad with a question in her eyes but spoke to Amanda. "I hope you return with Chad."

He nodded. "Yeah, I hope so, too."

Amanda couldn't make any promises. She wanted to get away before Kara reached for her again and she took her. Or broke into tears. She turned toward the door. "We need to go."

Outside, she couldn't stop the tears from filling her eyes and running down her cheeks. She walked ahead of Chad, hoping he wouldn't notice, while she tried to wipe them away. In the truck he started the engine and pulled onto the street. He didn't look at her but simply said, "I'm sorry. Do you feel like stopping for something to drink?"

"Yes, that's fine." Amanda wiped her eyes again and took a deep breath. "I didn't mean to get so emotional. Actually, I was hoping you wouldn't notice."

He pulled a box of tissues from the console and handed them to her with a grin. "I'm not blind. I just stink as an uncle."

She took the tissues and mopped up the effects of her tears. "No, you care and that makes you a good uncle. Right now, you care a little too much, and Kara senses that. When you relax around her, she'll know, and then she'll find out how wonderful you are."

As soon as the words left her mouth, she wished them back. "I mean as an uncle."

His grin let her know he'd caught her slip and enjoyed her discomfort. "Thanks. I appreciate your confidence in me. As an uncle, I mean."

She stuck her tongue out at him, and he chuckled. He drove to the drive-in and stopped beside a menu board. "So, what do you want?"

"Iced tea."

He placed the order and then turned toward Amanda. "I'm sorry I asked you to go."

"What?" He couldn't have said anything to hurt her more.

"I'm not sorry you went. I can't tell you how glad I am you were there. Linda told me about your baby. She was the same age, wasn't she?"

"Charity." Amanda whispered her baby's name. "Yes, she was ten months old when she died."

Tears threatened to fall again past Amanda's fragile control. Her emotions hovered near the surface, waiting to break free.

"I'm sorry. I can't even imagine how tough that had to be."

"I hope you never do." Amanda held a tissue to her eyes and then met his compassionate gaze. "I don't even know if you have children."

He gave a bitter-sounding laugh and looked out the windshield. "Nope, not a one. Except Kara. Here's our drinks."

⊷

Chad took the drinks and paid for them while Amanda used another tissue. He'd pulled her through a rosebush of memories today. Why did pain, like thorns, always seem to hide among love and beauty? How could a guy make up for stuff like that? She didn't blame him for today, but she blamed him for what happened back when they were engaged. He'd loved her so much and he still lost her. She'd already married some guy in California before he figured out what'd happened. He never found a way to tell her how they'd been manipulated. Of course, he'd already gone through a wedding ceremony before he fully understood.

He handed Amanda her tea and took a sip of his own. She was single now, same as him. Could this be a second chance for them? If things turned out the way he'd like over the summer, maybe he and Amanda could make a home together for Kara. Maybe they could have children of their own just as they'd planned long ago.

"I overheard some of the men talking after church Wednesday night about your barn." Her eyes shone as if the tears were still near the surface, but she didn't seem so close to the edge as she had a moment ago.

He breathed a little easier. "My cement floor, you mean?"

She nodded. "Yes, but maybe not for long. You teach history, don't you?"

He nodded, wondering what that had to do with anything.

Her quick laugh sounded like music to him. "Then you've surely heard of the old barn raisings the old folks used to do."

"Yeah." She had his interest. "What about it?"

"That's what they're talking about doing. I'm afraid they

may not come out for a couple of weeks, though. Pastor Mattson has a conference to attend and one of the couples who came out is also attending. If they didn't mention it to you this morning, I imagine they'll call you this week. How much more work is needed inside?"

He sighed, feeling the weight of his situation. "I wonder if there's that much hurry. Kara hates me. She's happy in the foster home. You saw that today."

"No, I didn't." Amanda sounded angry. "I saw a man who is scared of a baby and that's all I saw. When you get over your fear, she'll be fine. Now what's left before she can come home to you?"

He glanced at her and saw the sparks fly from her eyes. He grinned. This was the Amanda he remembered. "I still have to nail shingles to the roof. The windows are all in now, thanks to our retired carpenter. You and the other ladies did a great job in the house, but I'd like to have it cleaned. I mean in every room, and I'm not sure I can do that by myself. You all only worked in those rooms that had been hit. Then there's so much to go through. If I sell the house, I'll have to do something with the personal things. Do you understand what I'm talking about?"

Amanda nodded. "Yes. Will you sell, give away, store, what?"

He hadn't thought that far ahead. He grinned at her. "Want to help me decide?"

She stared at him with eyes as wary as Kara's had been. What? Didn't any female trust him? "Come on, Mandy, you know I don't bite. What's the problem? Didn't you say something about needing a summer job? Why don't you go to work for me? I'll pay you. I can afford it."

She laughed as if she didn't believe him. "On a teacher's salary?"

No, with proceeds from life insurance. Money he planned

to set aside for Kara, but some could be used to help bring her home. He didn't want to tell Amanda that, so he laughed along with her.

"When you've been teaching as long as I have, you'll find that a teacher can live on less than most people. That leaves a lot left over for savings. You don't know how wealthy I am."

Amanda giggled. "Yeah, sure."

He grinned. "Come on, Mandy. Please say you'll work for me. I'm serious when I say I can afford to pay you whatever you ask." His grin widened and he winked. "As long as it's no more than minimum."

She hesitated long enough he figured it wouldn't hurt to tip the scales in his favor, so he added, "If you won't do it for me, will you for Kara? Please say yes."

She closed her eyes and frowned as if in pain before she turned to look at him. "All right, Chad. When do you want me to report for duty?"

six

Monday morning Amanda checked on applications she'd turned in. Her cell phone rang as she left a discount store. Chad's voice responded to her greeting. "Hey, Amanda, guess what? I've got electricity. The truck just left."

"Congratulations." Why'd he call to tell her? And why did her heart jump every time she heard his voice? She breathed deep to calm the reaction she didn't want.

"So, do you feel up to a little housecleaning this afternoon?" He sounded happier than usual today. He chuckled. "Oh, there's another thing. You were right. Your pastor called and looks like we'll be having an old-fashioned barn raising out here."

"That's great, Chad." Amanda got in her mom's car and started it. "I've got transportation today, so I'll come out right after I get some lunch. Will that be okay?"

"What do you mean, you have transportation today? Whose car have you been driving?"

"Mom's. I sold mine in California before I moved."

"Aren't you going to buy another?"

She pulled out onto the street. "Yes, as soon as I get Dad motivated to help me look."

"I see." He dropped the subject then. "So I'll see you in a little bit. Can you stay for dinner? Food's a benefit of the job."

"I don't think so. Thanks anyway." Her heart couldn't pound harder if she'd been running.

"Oh, come on, Mandy." His voice pleaded. "Bring something to change into. You can even shower here if you want. We have water and electricity. Fully modern now.

We'll go someplace nice."

Rather than argue with him, she said, "I don't know, Chad. We'll see."

"Great, see you later then."

❧

Amanda drove to Chad's with dread and eager anticipation fighting for dominance in her emotions. She parked beside his truck in the wide driveway and went to the house. Chad's voice startled her.

"Hey, Mandy, I'm sure glad to see you." He walked from the barn site toward her. "Go on in, and if you need anything just holler. I'm trying to figure out how much lumber we'll need for a new barn. Some of this might be used again, but I'm no carpenter."

"Maybe Ron Kimbel could help you with that." She watched him move closer.

"I hate to bother anyone else, but looks like I'll have to if I plan to be ready for the barn raising." He grinned and stopped not far from the front porch. "You know, I'm really looking forward to that. Sounds like a lot of fun to me."

"It does." She laughed. "Mom's already thinking about what she plans to fix and bring. She mentioned it to Karen, and I wouldn't be surprised if she and Wayne come. Maybe Brad and Esther will, too."

"Have the whole clan here, huh?" His grin went straight to her heart, stirring memories she'd rather leave buried. "I haven't seen Brad in years."

"Yeah, you used to be friends." She didn't want to talk about the past with Chad. She turned toward the door and went inside.

He followed her. "Yep, Brad and Kevin Nichols. Remember him? We were probably the closest. Kevin and Sarah Maddox. I always thought they should've stayed together. Guess it wasn't meant to be. Everything blew up when she got pregnant."

Amanda smiled. "You haven't kept in touch with Kevin? I wondered if he'd send you an invitation."

"Invitation to what?" Chad frowned. "Last he knew I lived in Kentucky."

"Kentucky!" Amanda stared at him while a sick feeling stirred her stomach. How little she knew this man. Fourteen years had changed them both from the kids they'd been. They'd had experiences the other knew nothing about. Yet he was the same in many ways, and that familiarity drew her to learn about this older, cynical sounding Chad. "Why did you live in Kentucky? Did you teach school there?"

His laugh was short and bitter. "Yes, my first contract. My wife wanted to be close to her family. But what about Kevin? Invitation to what?"

She smiled. "Kevin and Sarah were married in August last year. They are expecting their first and probably last child already. Sarah said they'd wasted enough time and they both want this baby very much."

"First?" Chad quirked an eyebrow. "Don't you mean second?"

Amanda laughed. "Maybe a little of both. Trey's in college, and I think he seems more friend than child to them." She walked to the coffee table and ran her finger over the surface and looked at it. "Hmm. Not too bad. Do you want me to clean today or sort? You mentioned both."

"Would you mind cleaning?" The look in his eyes spoke of a vulnerability that shot straight to Amanda's heart. "The longer Kara's in foster care, the harder it's going to be for her to adjust to me. But bringing her back here where she's familiar with things might help. At least I hope it does."

"It will." Amanda touched his arm, and before she could pull back, he covered her hand with his.

"I appreciate what you're doing to help me, although I

sometimes wonder why you'd even bother speaking to me."

Amanda did pull back then. "Maybe we shouldn't talk about the past. We went separate ways and that's the way it should stay. I'm here to help, that's all, Chad."

"There are things you don't know, Mandy. Things I don't understand, but have a better idea now than I did then."

She swung to face him. "Look, you made your choices, and I made mine. Why don't we just drop the subject for now? I came today because of Kara. I want to see her home and settled. Let's concentrate on that."

Chad's expression hardened. "Sure Amanda, if that's the way you want it. For now. Maybe when she gets home, we'll have that talk."

He stepped to the door and stood with it open. "I need to finish shingling the roof. You know where everything is?"

She nodded and watched him leave. She stood for a moment, staring around the living room without seeing it while his words played through her mind. He wanted to talk about that night. She needed to hear his side of what happened. She'd already heard Susan's that night. But Susan married him. When had they married? Right after she left for California or years later? He'd said his first job was in Kentucky. Susan was from Kentucky. So they must have married right away. She'd refused to listen to any word about Chad or Susan back then, and she was doing the same now. What was she so afraid of?

She sighed and went into the utility room for the vacuum sweeper. Chad wanted a thorough cleaning. Maybe she could figure out the attachments and give the walls and ceiling a quick brush before starting on the floor.

Amanda had always enjoyed a challenge as long as she could see something accomplished. As she worked on the living room, she moved everything to one side and cleaned walls, ceiling, and floor before dusting and moving the furniture back into place.

Throughout the afternoon she tried to ignore the noises she heard on the roof and the man who made them. He came in the dining room door once to get a drink and helped her move the sofa back into place.

"It's looking good." He grinned. "You want something to drink? Water? Soda? We've got ice in the refrigerator now."

"Sure." She walked ahead of him and fixed a glass of ice water for herself. "How about you?"

He snagged a can of root beer. "This is fine for me." He pulled a chair from the kitchen table and sat down as if he planned to stay.

After a long cooling drink, she set her glass on the counter and headed out of the room. "I need to get back to work."

She felt his gaze until she reached the living room and heard him go back outside. She started working on the second side of the room. It wasn't right for Chad to have such an effect on her emotions after so long. Had she forgotten Jeff and the love they'd shared?

She dusted the coffee table and set it in place. Jeff seemed so long gone. She remembered the week before the accident. They'd gone to the beach one afternoon and walked along the shore. They stopped and helped Charity build a sand castle of sorts. She smiled. Neither of them was very artistic. But the memory was good. Of the castle and Charity patting it to the ground as quickly as they built it.

She sank to the sofa and tried to bring Jeff's face from her memory. Like a will-o'-the-wisp, the image she wanted floated just outside her grasp. When Chad's features popped with clarity into her mind, she stood and cried out, "No."

How could she forget Jeff? Even worse, how could she replace him with a man who had been unfaithful to her? A man who had broken her heart once and could easily do it again if she didn't keep her distance? She shoved her thoughts away and worked harder than ever to keep them from returning. After the last piece of furniture was in place, she stood back with her arms crossed and admired the clean room. She was tired, but content that she'd done a good job.

"Is it safe to come inside?" Chad stood in the open doorway between the living room and dining room, a hesitant look on his face.

Amanda crossed her arms and faced him. "I'm just the hired help. You don't need my permission."

He grinned. "I do if you're thinking of throwing something at me."

"Like I would do such a thing."

His chuckle reached inside and touched a longing that had to be wrong. She ignored it and lifted her chin. "Are you laughing at me?"

He lifted his hand and waved it while he shook his head. "Oh no, not me. I was just thinking."

"About what?"

"Oh, that time you threw your shoe at me." He looked toward the ceiling as if thinking. "And do you remember the dog?"

She opened her eyes wide. "I never threw a—" Her hand covered her mouth. "Oh, but that wasn't a real dog. It was ceramic. And I never hit you." She giggled. "In fact, I don't think I've ever hit anything in my life."

"Tell that to the dog." He laughed. "And the door that broke it into a million pieces."

She lifted her eyebrows. "And your point is?"

"I don't have a point." He grinned. "I like having you here. Seems like I've been alone most of my life, but I never realized how lonely alone can be until you stepped out of your car a week ago. Didn't know how much I've missed you all these years, either."

"Yeah, like a wart." He drew her in with his words and the

memories that seemed as if they'd happened yesterday. She couldn't let him do that to her. She couldn't let him hurt her again. Maybe she should let him talk about the past. Maybe it was time to understand what had really happened between them. Why he had turned to another woman within weeks of their wedding. Why he had broken her heart.

"No, never a wart, Mandy." His voice grew soft. "More like a beautiful woman who's going to go take a shower now and dress for dinner with me. You did bring a change of clothes, didn't you?"

She shook her head and his smile wavered.

He shrugged. "Then go home and get ready. I'll pick you up there."

She sighed. "Oh, all right."

She turned, but not before she saw his eyes light up and the smile return that always set her heart tripping in time. She was in trouble and she knew it, but she couldn't stop now. She wanted to go to dinner with Chad. She wanted just this one night to relive a time that had been jerked from her grasp.

seven

Two hours later, Amanda sat in Chad's truck while he drove north toward Springfield. She shouldn't be here. What did she think she was doing?

"Do you have a favorite restaurant you'd like to go to?" Chad spoke over the music from his CD player.

She tried to remember the places they'd gone to back in college but could think of only one. "What about Martinels? They used to have pretty decent food."

Something flickered in his eyes, but he nodded. "Sounds good to me if they're still in business."

"They should be. There's been a lot of promotion for Historic Route 66 lately and they're sitting pretty close to it."

"Yeah, I've noticed."

A shiver chased down her spine. Route 66 had played an important role recently in her friends' lives. Tessa reconnected with her son's father because she decided to travel the old road. Sarah said Kevin used the road as the base from which to re-win her heart. He even proposed to her near the beginning of Route 66. First Tessa, and then Sarah, had been brought together with the one man she couldn't forget. Was she next?

No, that couldn't be. Amanda turned off the inner voice that mocked her with possibilities she believed were impossible. Long ago she'd forgiven Chad for what he'd done, but how could she ever forget?

"I guess you haven't been back this way much." She needed conversation to keep her imagination quiet. "I usually only got home once a year. Karen lives in Springfield, but other than a short visit when she picked me up at the airport, I always stayed with Mom and Dad. But Jessica must have drawn you to this part of the state once in a while."

He nodded. "Yeah, we tried to get together for the holidays and maybe once during the summer." His jaw clenched. "If I'd known what would happen, I'd have made the trip a whole lot more. At least maybe then Kara would know me."

"She'll get acquainted, Chad. Just give her a little time. When Karen's oldest daughter was that age, she screamed every time Brad tried to play with her. It really hurt his feelings, but he kept trying. Now she thinks he's the greatest uncle ever. She tags along after him any time they get together."

In an obvious attempt to change the subject, Chad said, "The old road went through every town, large or small, didn't it? We're on Historic 66 now. No wonder it didn't last. Those people must have gone at a snail's crawl back then. We're too impatient nowadays."

"Yes, that's what I've been trying to tell you." Amanda gave him a pointed look and smiled at the guilt that crossed his face. She laughed. "You and Kara are going to be inseparable before long. I can feel it."

"Yeah, I bet." He slowed and turned on his blinker. "Looks like we're about there."

All right, she wouldn't say anything more about Kara.

They were seated at a candlelit table for two waiting for their dinner when Chad said, "You know the museum is just down the road from here."

Amanda smiled. "I remember. Abraham Lincoln Presidential Library and Museum. It was one of your favorite hangouts."

"Maybe we could go again sometime and check it out. See if there's anything new or something we missed." He grinned at her.

"Chad"—she shook her head—"I doubt you missed anything. Now me, maybe."

"Your favorite subject was English, I know." He made a face. "I never could understand why anyone would rather write an essay than study out the facts of specific times in our history. Our lives today are what they are because of the events of the past."

"Yes, Mr. Randall." Amanda laughed. "But you never seemed to mind when I helped you write a paper for class, did you? Remember all those good grades you got?"

He chuckled, but something in the depths of his eyes reached into her and tugged on her heart. "You were good for me, Mandy. We made a great team. We still do. After all this time, you're still helping me."

"Temporarily." Amanda let that one word stand between them as she turned toward the waitress arriving with a large plate in each hand. "Looks like our food is here."

&

Chad watched Amanda take a sip of water and set the glass back. He could scarcely believe he sat across from his Mandy after all this time. He'd thought he was dreaming when he recognized her in Jessica's front yard. He'd been afraid to speak to her but had managed a few words. He loved that she'd gone to see Kara with him, and to see her in the house and looking so at home today was more than he'd ever expected. Now, being with her at the restaurant where they'd gone the night he'd proposed was truly beyond belief. Did she remember? Maybe they could erase the last fourteen years and begin again. But first, he'd have to open some painful wounds and convince her to let him talk.

"I don't think this restaurant has changed at all." Amanda looked around the dining area.

Several tables were filled. A young couple sat at one. There were a few older couples, but just as it used to be, several tables were taken by college-aged people.

He nodded. "It does look the same. Do you remember the last time we were here?"

Her eyes darkened and a flush touched her cheeks. She remembered.

She looked down at her plate. "We came more than once, Chad, and it was a long time ago."

"I'm only asking about the last time." He pushed because he hated sweeping what they had into a dark corner where it could be forgotten. "I can't forget, Mandy. I won't. Just as our country's past affects us today, our personal past makes us the adults we are. We have hurts in our past, and we need to take them out and talk about them so they can heal. So we can heal."

Her gaze met his, and he felt as if he could get lost in the emerald depths of her eyes. His beautiful, sweet Mandy. If only she'd let him tell her what he suspected. Maybe she could confirm what he thought he knew.

"Some things are better left in the past." Her voice sounded soft and uncertain.

He hesitated, not wanting to run her off. "Let's enjoy our meal, our time together. We'll talk later."

She visibly relaxed as she smiled at him. "That's a good idea. And we will talk, Chad. I want to know and understand, too. It's just hard for me, although I don't know why that should be. You'd think fourteen years would be long enough."

She didn't say long enough for what, but Chad knew. Long enough to cover the pain. Long enough to forget. He'd never forgotten her, and now he knew he never would.

They ate baked potato wedges and fried fish while they talked about everything except the one subject they both wanted to avoid but couldn't forget. Finally Chad had to at least skirt the edge. "Tell me about your husband. What was his name? Where'd you meet him?"

Her eyes became wary, but she blotted her lips with the napkin and answered. "Jeffrey. We met at church."

"Will you tell me about it?" He'd be hurt in the telling, but he had to know.

"I went to California to live with my cousin and went to the church she and her family attended. The Wilsons were members of the church, too. His parents and my cousins still are. Jeff was a junior at the university there. We married not long after we met, and I worked while he finished his degree."

"So you didn't go back to school?" Why couldn't he ask if she'd loved her husband since that's what he really wanted to know?

She shook her head. "Not until about a year after the accident."

"Can you talk about the accident?" He knew she meant the car accident that took her husband's and her daughter's lives. "Were you injured?"

She nodded but stared at her plate. "I had internal injuries as well as some broken bones. I was either in the hospital or in therapy for over a year."

"Oh Mandy." No words described the pain he felt knowing she had suffered so much. "I'm sorry."

She did meet his gaze then, and she smiled. "No, don't be. Jeff and Charity are at home with the Lord. Many of our darkest moments are a tool God uses to bring us closer to Him if we allow Him to. I lost so much then, but I gained, too. I'm stronger now than before. I'm closer to the Lord than I've ever been, and I'm learning every day to rely on Him. He holds me in the palm of His hand. If He leaves me here to walk with Him or takes me home tonight, I know I'm safe."

Chad watched the sparkle in her eyes as she talked, and

he sensed she meant exactly what she said. She held no bitterness toward God for taking her husband and child. He'd like to know her secret. How could she give up the ones she loved and say all was fine? Surely she loved her baby, but did she love Jeffrey?

"You're a better person than I am. Always were." He stared at his plate.

She laughed. "Hardly. I'm the spoiled baby of the family. Just ask my older brother and sister, if you don't believe me."

He looked up with a smile. "Naw, I'll take your word for it. Remember, I've seen you in action."

"What a terrible thing to say." She slapped at him and hit air. "You owe me for that."

"Oh? And what will pay for my transgression?" He chuckled, glad the heavy conversation had ended.

"You asked about my husband." She searched his face, her eyes holding him captive. "Now, it's your turn. I was told you married Susan. When did that happen and how?"

He choked when a piece of fish tried to go down the wrong way. He coughed and took a long swallow of water before it settled into the right passage. "Sorry, but I wasn't expecting that."

"You don't want to tell me?" She challenged him.

"It's a time I'd rather forget, but you're right. You need to know." He looked across the table at her and wished he could erase Susan from his past. "We had a wedding ceremony about a month after you left. How did it happen that I agreed to marry someone like Susan? That's simple, if not honorable. She convinced me she was carrying my child."

eight

Amanda lost the ability to speak or think. Her world froze in time and space with only Chad's face within her vision. She saw pain and more in his eyes. Regret? Shame? Sorrow? Guilt? His gaze never wavered. Hers didn't either.

He covered her hand with his. "Mandy, let's go somewhere private and talk. If you'll listen, I'd like to tell you everything as I know it. Susan deceived both of us."

"Susan deceived us?" She spat out the words, her voice scarcely more than a whisper, yet loud with emotion. "She obviously wasn't the only one."

"Please, Amanda." Chad stood and tugged on her hand. "We need to talk this out. I want you to know everything before you start blaming only one of us."

"Before I blame you." She let him help her stand only because she didn't want to create a scene. Yet.

She waited while Chad paid for the food that now sat as a heavy lump in her stomach. She allowed him to open and hold her door while she got in the truck. Neither spoke while he drove to a nearby park and stopped. Chad lowered their windows and turned off the lights along with the engine. He sat in the dark silence, staring straight ahead as if he saw what Amanda could only imagine.

When he didn't speak right away, the darkness pressed against her. She had to know what he saw. She'd waited for answers far too long. "Where's Susan now?"

"I don't know."

Chad's whispered answer hit Amanda like a yell. She pushed back into the corner of the seat against the door.

"Why? Are you divorced?"

"No."

She shrank even farther from him. "You're still married?"

He shook his head. The torment in his eyes tore through her. "I never married Susan. I only thought I did."

"You're making no sense." She fumbled for the door handle. She couldn't breathe. She had to get away.

His hand closed over her arm. "Amanda, wait. Let me tell you all of it. Will you listen?"

Something in his tone calmed her. She nodded and he removed his hand.

"I stupidly believed Susan. She set up the wedding. We each had a witness. Kevin stood up with me. We signed the papers and the minister took them. I didn't know until she left me that she'd hired a fake minister. He not only wasn't ordained, he wasn't even a minister. Just a good actor who needed his next fix. At least that's what she told me the day she left."

Amanda made a disgusted sound. "And you believed her?"

"Not really. I checked with the county, and sure enough, there was no record of our marriage. It was a sham. She used me and tossed me aside when there was no need."

"Why would she need a husband? She had no morals."

Chad gave a quick laugh. "True enough, but her father did. Her father was very strict and quite wealthy. If she'd had a child outside marriage, he'd have cut her off."

Amanda looked into his eyes. Surely Chad wouldn't make up such a story. He'd never been deceptive. Had Susan deceived them both as he claimed? But she'd seen him with Susan, and he'd admitted there was a baby. The bitter thought left a sour taste in her soul, and she covered her lips with her fingers and pressed hard.

"I'm sorry, Mandy." Chad's gentle voice surrounded her. "I've wanted to tell you for days. The timing never seemed right. That's one reason I wanted us to go out tonight.

There's so much to say. Will you listen to the rest?"

He turned to face her, watching her. She looked across the cab at him. The streetlight scarcely illuminated the inside of the truck, but she could see Chad well enough to know this wasn't easy for him either. She should be angry at him. Angry and shocked as she'd felt in the restaurant, but somehow those emotions had evaporated, leaving a numb acceptance instead. Now she felt detached, as if the story of Chad's life didn't affect her.

She nodded. "What about your child? Why did you tell me you had no children?"

"I never had a child." Chad shrugged. "That's another of Susan's deceptions."

What was he trying to pull? His words cut like thorns scraping her heart. She choked out the accusation she'd held inside for fourteen years. "That isn't true. I saw you, Chad. I saw the two of you together in the park that night."

As she said the words, the realization hit with enough force that she gasped. "It was this very park. How could you do that? Chad, how could you bring me here of all places to talk about Susan and you? Don't you know I loved you?"

"You loved me then, Mandy, and I loved you. But Susan and I didn't do what you think. Not that night. That was another of her deceptions. Oh, there were many." His voice sounded bitter as if he'd like to spit the words out and be done with them. "She played us both for fools that night. She was your good friend telling me you'd sent her here to talk to me. To tell me it was over between us. I was hurt beyond reason and she took advantage of that, consoling me. The hug you saw was only that, Amanda. Only a hug."

"You were all over her." Amanda's eyes burned and she swiped at them. She would not cry another tear over Chad. Not now. Not after what he'd done. "I know what I saw. Besides, she told me what happened."

"She lied to you." Chad's quick harsh laugh told his feelings. "Let me guess. Did she tell you I came on to her? Did she tell you I asked her to meet me here?"

"No, she said you just showed up and told her you wanted to call our wedding off. She said you'd been having second thoughts. Then she said you came on to her. You seduced her. Where's the deception, Chad? I saw you when I got here."

"And why did you come? Who invited you? Susan? I think I understand better now. She told you to meet her here at the park at a certain time, didn't she? But why would you? What did she want to tell you that had to be said in a secluded spot where no one else would hear? Things about me? Maybe the same things she told you after giving her performance with me. A performance, I might add, that I fell for because my heart was torn in two at the time." His voice lowered. "I'd just been convinced that the woman I loved more than my own life wanted out. She said you'd been talking about going to California."

"For a visit, not to live." Amanda's head spun. She didn't know what to think. "I told Susan I'd been invited to California. I never said I was going. I wouldn't have gone if you and Susan hadn't. . ."

"Amazing, isn't it, how different the truth is from what we've believed all these years. Susan should have been the one who went to California. She'd been a better actress than she was a pretend wife." Chad sounded bitter and Amanda was beginning to believe him.

"I don't understand all this, Chad. There are parts missing. How about your baby? You aren't so gullible to believe that unless there was cause."

A deep sigh tore from him. "I'm sorry, Mandy. You can't imagine how sorry I am. I've regretted my weakness from the night it happened. But please believe me when I say nothing happened until after you left. Susan said she'd talk to you that night. I believed her and waited until the next day to see you, but you'd already gone home. I tried to call you. No one would let me talk to you. I drove to your house and Brad met me outside. He said you'd gone to California just like Susan said you'd planned. Why wouldn't I believe everything she told me by then?"

As he talked, pieces of the puzzle began to fall into place, and the pain in Amanda's chest lessened. She nodded encouragement.

"She became my friend, I thought. She sympathized and held me while I cried for you. No one else knew how much you'd hurt me. I took comfort in her arms and about a week after you'd gone, I lost control. Looking back now, I know Susan orchestrated the entire thing. From breaking us up to seducing me while I had no defense. That's no excuse, but that is what happened. I should've been stronger. There was only that night, but when she came to me a month later and said she would be having my baby, I figured one time was all it took. She arranged the wedding ceremony right away, but her baby was Down syndrome and died. If he'd lived, I'm not sure what would've happened. The poor little guy didn't have much of a chance either way."

Amanda frowned. "Maybe you could've gotten custody."

Chad's lips lifted in a mocking smile. "The baby was full-term, but we were together little more than six months when he was born. He wasn't mine, Amanda. I could've never proved he was. She used us for her own purposes. I'll never understand why she picked me. She certainly didn't care anything for me."

The truck cab was dark and silent as if they were cocooned within their own world. Amanda tried to process what Chad told her. Had Susan only pretended to be her friend? She searched Chad's face and eyes and saw sincerity. He told the truth.

"Yeah, it's true. Every word." Chad spoke as if he'd read her mind, which wasn't so hard to imagine. He'd done that before. He turned the ignition key and his truck roared to life. "I'll take you home, Amanda. It's getting late."

She nodded, unable to think beyond the idea of what Susan had done. Amanda looked at the park while Chad backed his truck out and pulled away. It had been late that night when Susan set her trap for Chad. She got them both to the park to witness a scene of her own making. Oh, she'd been clever. Yet, in the long run, she'd lost so much. But so had Chad.

"I'm sorry, Amanda." Chad's voice in the silent cab startled Amanda.

She turned toward him. "I need time to think about all of this, but one thing I believe now is that you weren't totally at fault. You'd never done anything to make me think you'd been unfaithful. Susan knew that, and she set up a scene to convince me. I shouldn't have believed it even then."

"I'm sure she explained everything thoroughly." Chad's voice was bitter.

"Yes, she did. In fact, she thanked me for showing up when I did." Amanda turned toward the window when tears burned her eyes. She squeezed them away but couldn't stop the emotions that roiled in her chest. Her breath quickened as she relived that night. "Susan started crying before we got back to the dorm. She said if I hadn't come along when I did, she didn't know what might've happened."

At Chad's sudden intake of air, Amanda turned to look at him. His jaw clenched and he shook his head. "I thought she was your friend. I trusted her and look where it got me."

Amanda's head ached from an emotional turmoil she thought she'd put in her past. She hadn't expected this and didn't fully know how to handle what Chad had revealed. Their conversation drifted into silence as Chad turned his truck south toward Litchfield. She watched the dark countryside drift past as they rode on the highway. She saw a road sign that said they were on I-55, and a little farther another said Historic Route 66. How interesting when the past and the present blended together to make one road. She wondered if her life, hers and Chad's, were like the old road. Once Route 66 had flourished with life and purpose. Now the old road had been changed, torn apart in many places and rebuilt into something else so the Mother Road was scarcely recognizable. Isn't that what had happened to her dreams and even to her life? Chad, too, had changed from the innocent boy he'd been fourteen years ago. He'd been torn apart by deceit and manipulation until his basic beliefs had taken a beating. The loss of his sister and brother-in-law only added to his bitterness. Was there hope? As Route 66 had accepted the new, safer freeways across its miles, could she and Chad learn from their past and forge a new relationship or, at least, a new friendship?

They didn't talk on the drive home, but Amanda's thoughts churned. When Chad stopped in front of her parents' darkened house, she turned to him. "Thanks for telling me, Chad. I needed to know."

He simply smiled and opened his door. "You're welcome."

She waited while he circled the truck. They walked without touching to the front door where Chad grinned at her. "You aren't locked out, are you?"

She laughed, glad for a break in the tension that had gone on long enough. "You have a good memory, only this time I have my own key."

His grin disappeared as he looked into her eyes. "My memory isn't so good except where you're concerned. I've never been able to forget you, Mandy."

She searched for words and could find none. Then his attention centered on her mouth, and she knew he wouldn't wait for her response. He moved closer, giving her time to back away, but she couldn't move except to lift her face toward his. She watched the distance close, and his lips brushed hers in a short, friendly kiss that left her wishing things were different between them.

He opened the door for her and she stepped inside. "I'll see you tomorrow, Mandy. Good night."

She could only nod and watch him walk away.

❧

Throughout the rest of the week, Amanda drove to Chad's house each day and cleaned. By Friday she'd worked her way into the bedrooms and was vacuuming when Chad came inside. He spoke as soon as she turned the cleaner off.

"Hey, this place is looking real good."

"It is, isn't it?" She smiled at him. "Maybe ready for a little girl to come home?"

He frowned. "I finished the roof, the glass is all cleaned up, Rick came out yesterday and inspected. He says the house is solid. He didn't find any other problems. The barn still needs to be rebuilt."

"She won't be living in the barn, Chad."

"I know." He sighed. "She'll have to live in the house with me."

"And what's wrong with that?" As soon as the words left her mouth, Amanda wished she could call them back.

Chad's eyes darkened as they searched her face, as if he looked for a truth she didn't want revealed. Maybe he was right. Maybe she had been holding her emotions in check, keeping them private from him. Neither had mentioned Susan or the night they'd split up since their outing in Springfield and their confidences at the park. They also hadn't mentioned the kiss that night or how unsatisfactory it had been. Amanda wanted more than friendship. Maybe Chad didn't. Maybe she shouldn't read more into Chad's expression than his concern for his niece.

"Will the social worker come and inspect the house first?"

"Before Kara can come home?" His gaze shifted, and the intense expression on his face lifted as a wry smile took its place. "Oh yes, you can count on it."

Amanda knew the house would pass inspection. She straightened the cheerful Sunbonnet Sue quilt she'd smoothed over Kara's bed. Someone had sewn love with careful stitches into the small cover with bright patches of colorful fabric in the dresses and matching bonnets. "You don't need to worry about an inspection. It's just a matter of time, then."

"Yeah, the house is ready." He leaned against the door frame as if he didn't feel comfortable coming all the way into the room. "I can't decide if I want time to speed up or slow down. I'm going to see her Sunday afternoon again. If I come to church will you sit with me? We could go get something to eat and then visit with her."

Amanda gripped the bed railing for support. Did she want a baby she couldn't have to become part of her life? Her arms and her heart remembered how precious Kara felt as she snuggled close. How could she put herself through the bittersweet torture of holding Kara? Through the longing to have her own child when she knew it couldn't be? Yet, how could she walk away from the one thing she wanted more than anything else? A family of her own.

She wasn't so naive as to think she and Chad could pick up where they'd left off. Too many years with too many hurts had gone before. But they could be friends, and friends helped each other. Life couldn't get any simpler than that. Chad had a need and she helped with the house. Would it hurt so much to help him learn he had nothing to fear from Kara?

"Almost every Sunday after church my brother comes for

dinner. Sometimes Karen comes down, too. You are welcome if you don't mind eating with us." She waited as he stared across the room toward the window.

When he spoke, his voice was low. "I remember. I doubt your folks would want me there. Brad maybe, but not the rest."

"Brad and Karen. As for my parents, maybe you don't know them as well as you think you do." She unplugged the vacuum cleaner and wound the cord in place. "They don't hold grudges. I'm not sure they ever believed you did wrong in the first place. I'm the one with that problem."

"What about now, Mandy?" He stepped into the room and took the vacuum cleaner handle from her. "It's a matter of trust, isn't it? Who do you trust is telling the truth, Susan or me?"

Emotion clogged her throat, but she spoke around it. "I've never known you to lie, Chad."

He started to say more when his cell phone rang. Amanda took the vacuum cleaner and pushed it from the room while he talked. She stored the cleaner in the utility room and walked through the house admiring her week's work of cleaning. The house looked and smelled good. Kara could come home at any time. Chad needed to talk to the social worker and get the ball rolling.

"That was the lumberyard in Litchfield." Chad spoke from behind her. "They're bringing a load out for the barn. I'll talk to Pastor Mattson Sunday morning and see when they can come for the barn raising."

Amanda turned and saw his wide grin. He looked the happiest she'd seen him since the tornado. She couldn't help smiling, too. "Sounds like fun. I hope Kara is home by then. I was just thinking you should call and get an inspection of the house. Tell them you're ready to bring her home."

His grin disappeared, but he nodded. "I'll do that. Today."

"Good. Now why don't you show me what you want packed away, and I'll get started on that Monday?"

A sigh tore from him as he looked around the room. "I guess it all has to go by the end of summer. We need to start with the closets. I don't want to drag stuff out now until after the social worker is satisfied. I'd better call her now."

While he talked on the phone, Amanda went into the kitchen and opened a cabinet door. Jessica had plenty of dishes. Probably a lot more than Chad and Kara needed. Maybe she could start here. Would Chad want to keep everything, sell it, or give it away? She'd have to ask.

"Well, it's set." Chad walked up behind her and leaned against the counter, his arms crossed. "She'll be here Thursday afternoon."

"Kara?" Amanda's heart lost a beat.

"No, social services." A frown pulled the corners of his mouth down. "Kara stays until they decide, but I've got to go see her Sunday afternoon. Do some more bonding."

If he'd been heading for the gallows, he couldn't have looked more frightened. "Still need the company?"

Her offer visibly wiped the stress away as if a cloth had moved over his face leaving a smile in its place. "Would you, please?"

Amanda smiled and nodded. What else could she do? Her heart, her very life, had been captured by this man long ago and more recently by his sweet niece. If Jeff and Charity had lived, everything would be different. But she was alone now, and her love for Chad had never truly died. That truth hit her with bittersweet knowledge because love wasn't enough. She could scarcely wait until the day Kara came home to stay. Yet she wanted to prolong the time before then because, after Chad and Kara truly bonded, she would no longer be needed.

She shoved away from the counter and walked away. "I'll go home then and see you Sunday."

"How about tomorrow? We could go car shopping."

Amanda swung back to search his face. "For me?"

He chuckled. "Yes, for you. I don't need a car."

"That would be great." She laughed with him. "Thank you, Chad."

nine

Saturday morning Amanda directed Chad to Bob Larson Motors, a used car dealer in Litchfield where her dad had bought his truck and her mom's car. "This is where I saw what I want."

Their shoes crunched through the graveled lot to a dark blue compact car. Chad opened the driver's door and gave a quick look inside, pulled a lever that popped the hood, and then stepped around to lift it. Amanda watched him touch a wire where it attached to the motor then move on to something else that she couldn't identify. He bent over the fender, and she wondered if he'd crawl inside to see better if he could. The thought made her giggle.

He turned his head to look at her and grinned. "Are you laughing at me or the car?"

"Both." She couldn't stop her smile any more than she could turn away from his.

"Mornin', folks." Bob Larson stopped in front of the car. "Hi, Amanda. I didn't realize that was you. How're you doin'?"

"Fine. Bob, this is Chad Randall. He knows more about cars than I do and offered to help me find one." As Chad straightened, Amanda said, "Chad, Bob goes to the same church as my folks. We always look here first for cars."

The men shook hands and Chad said, "Amanda's already picked this one out for looks. What can you tell me about it?"

Amanda listened to the car's history, but let Chad ask the questions. They walked around the car checking for dents and scratches, inspected the tires, and looked in the trunk.

She wanted to sit behind the wheel and see how it drove, so she was glad when Bob made the suggestion. "Let me go get the keys and you can take it for a spin."

"That would be great."

Amanda drove to her parents' house and stopped in the driveway. Chad gave her a questioning look. "Are you hoping for a second opinion?"

She released her seat belt. "Wouldn't do any good. No one's home."

Before he could respond, she hopped out, ran around the car, and opened his door. "Don't you want to drive?"

He grinned and swiped his hand across his brow. "Whew, I thought for a minute you were going to throw me to the lions."

"Mom and Dad?" She laughed. "Maybe Daddy, but Mom always thought I made a mistake."

As soon as the words popped out of her mouth, she wished she could recall them. He stepped from the car and towered over her. She stepped back. He stepped forward and caught her hands. "Mandy, what do you think?"

She gave him an innocent look. "I like the way it drives, but I'd like to know what you think, too."

"What I think?"

She breathed easier and nodded.

He looked deep into her eyes. "I think we both made some stupid mistakes, but God has given us a second chance. I think it would be another stupid mistake to ignore what's going on between us right now."

"Chad." She put as much warning in her voice as she could. He couldn't mean what he'd said. He only wanted her to help him with Kara. Too many years had passed to heal all the hurts they'd caused each other. All the damage Susan had done to their relationship. "Let's just look at the car. Please? We're friends now. I don't want to ruin that."

He gave a short, bitter laugh but released her hands. "Yeah, Amanda, we're friends."

He left her to get in the car and went around to the driver's side. They didn't speak again until Chad pulled into the lot and parked. Then he turned toward her. "If you want this car, I think it's fine." He shrugged. "The price is right, the tires look almost new, and I can't find any problems."

She nodded. "Thanks, Chad. I really appreciate this. Mom will be glad to have her car back."

Amanda wrote a check for the full amount of the car and drove it home. Chad followed her to the house, and she thought he might come in, but he only stopped at the curb long enough to remind her he'd see her the next day. As he drove away, loss for what she'd once almost had pressed against her heart.

Chad wanted more than friendship. Why did that scare her? Why couldn't she forget the hurt Susan had caused? Chad said he was innocent and she believed him. She loved Jeffrey, but he'd been gone for years. She couldn't cling to his memory forever. She felt ready to move on, to find someone who would love her in spite of her inability to bear children. Just not Chad. She couldn't do that to him. She loved him too much.

She let herself into the house as the full implication of her reluctance hit her full force. She loved Chad. Whether her love had never died or she'd fallen in love all over again, she didn't know. But the love that burned in her heart at that moment was real and the realization tore through her.

She shoved the door closed with enough force to rattle the window. Why had this happened? She'd ignored him for years, refusing to listen to anything pertaining to him or Susan. She hurt so much from the love she'd lost. Now they'd been thrown together to be hurt again. Her heart ached.

She ran upstairs to her room where she'd always sought

solace from life's problems. There she sat on her bed and picked up her Bible. *Lord, please give me direction. Show me what to do about Chad. Does he know You? He says You're giving us a second chance. Is that what this is all about? You know I can't have children.* Tears filled her eyes.

If Chad is innocent like he says, he deserves better. He thought he'd married Susan because there was a child. Surely he wants children and I can't. I just can't.

Tears fell from her weeping heart and she clutched her Bible close.

　　　　　ᴥ

Chad sat beside Amanda at church Sunday morning and wondered if God had truly brought them back together. He'd never stopped loving her. Even when he thought he was married, he couldn't let go of his memories. He heard little of the sermon and was glad when church ended so they could slip outside to his truck.

"Are you coming to Mom and Dad's for dinner?" Amanda's green eyes sparkled and he figured she knew he'd turn the invitation down.

"How about I buy you a quick lunch instead so we can spend more time with Kara?" He watched one expression after another chase through her eyes. They came alive with an eager light that quickly dimmed.

If he could read her mind, would he find that she missed her little girl and maybe her husband, too? The idea brought a surge of jealousy followed by shame. How could he be jealous of a man who'd been dead for years? So he'd married Mandy. That shouldn't matter. Even if she'd loved him. Only it did matter. If not to him, to her. Was that why she held back? Because she still loved her husband?

The expression in her eyes softened and she smiled. "Sure, Chad, I'll let you off the hook this time, but sooner or later, you'll have to have dinner with us. Brad will be back from vacation tomorrow, and he won't let you get away with all these excuses, so you may as well plan on next week."

Chad laughed. "Okay, I'll plan on it. Maybe I'll have Kara then. Actually, did I tell you Kara will be eating with us today?"

The smile in her eyes lit her entire face and Chad's heart. "No. Why didn't you say that in the first place?"

"Maybe it was supposed to be a surprise." He grinned at her as he closed her door and ran around to the driver's side.

On the way to Lakeland, they talked about nothing important, but Chad could have listened to Amanda's voice forever. She belonged in his truck and in his life. She always had. If he had his way, she always would.

Kara reached for Amanda as soon as she saw her. She patted Amanda's cheek and tilted her head while she babbled a string of unintelligible words that obviously had meaning to her. Amanda laughed and hugged her close. "Oh, sweetheart, has it only been one week? It seems like forever since I saw you last."

Kara laid her head on Amanda's shoulder and looked so at home Chad felt a lump form in his throat. Still, his smile came easily as they headed to his truck. He held the door while Amanda buckled Kara in the car seat then sat in front.

"All set?"

She nodded so he closed the door. When he slid behind the steering wheel, he asked, "How would you like a picnic? We can get chicken with mashed potatoes at the deli. Do you think she can eat chicken?"

"If we tear it into small pieces."

He nodded. "Good. We'll go to the park."

"Let's do it." Amanda's smile showed her approval.

❧

By the time he pulled to a stop near the city park, Chad looked forward to this outing. Amanda took charge of Kara and that suited him fine. Kara seemed happy. He wondered at the way Kara and Amanda had bonded, almost as if each supplied a need in the other's life. And they probably did. Amanda needed this time with Kara to ease the hurt from her own baby as much as Kara needed the mothering she found in Amanda. At least that made sense to him. If only the connection could be permanent.

"I brought a quilt from the house. I'll get it for you and Kara and then bring everything else while you keep her corralled." Chad soon had a quilt spread over the grass near the playground and brought the bags of food.

"Pretty quiet here." He looked from the deserted park back to Amanda. "We're the only ones here."

"For now." She smiled. "It's still early in the afternoon. Everyone gets around a little slower on Sunday."

"You're probably right." Chad sat on the quilt and began pulling their dinner from the bags.

Amanda seemed content to take care of Kara. He could watch them together all day. This scene had been his dream fourteen years ago, only he'd pictured Mandy with their child. He still couldn't think of Kara as his; although as time went by, no doubt he would become more father than uncle to her. If only he could convince Amanda to be her mother.

As they finished eating, a couple of kids ran into the park and jumped on the merry-go-round. Their voices calling to each other caught Kara's attention. She sat on the quilt beside Amanda watching with wide eyes until a smile broke across her face. She clapped her hands and squealed.

Amanda laughed.

Chad's heart swelled within his chest. They were his. Kara of necessity, Mandy by a love that refused to die. If only he could convince her it was still there for both of them.

Amanda's laughing eyes met his. "I think she wants to play with the big kids."

A protective surge he hadn't expected swept through him, and he shook his head. "Not on that thing. She'd get hurt. There's a baby swing. You want to see if she'll like it?"

"If you help." Amanda's eyes held a challenge.

She started gathering their trash and handed it to him to throw away. As soon as they had everything picked up, she stood with Kara. Chad shook out the quilt and took it to his truck. When he returned, Amanda was fastening Kara in the swing. She turned toward him and stepped back with a smile. "You can take it from here."

"And make her cry," Chad muttered under his breath.

Amanda heard and laughed. "Stay behind her until she gets used to you. She doesn't care who pushes her swing, just so it keeps going."

Chad began to relax when Amanda moved in front of the swing where Kara could see her and she could play with her. All he had to do was provide the power. After a while, Amanda traded places with him and Kara laughed and squealed when he acted like he might catch her. They played for quite a while until Amanda caught the swing and slowed it to a stop.

"Don't we need to be getting back?" She started unbuckling the belt that held Kara in the swing as she talked to her, telling her that they had to stop swinging now.

"Yeah, you're right. Playtime's over." Chad moved closer to Amanda and Kara let out a wail that pierced his heart. "What'd I do now?"

Amanda laughed. "Nothing. She doesn't want to stop."

Chad stepped back and watched Amanda disengage the seat belt while Kara's hands continually got in the way, trying to hook it back into place. Her cries grew louder while Amanda talked to her in a calm but firm voice.

"No, Kara. I know you want to swing more, but we have to go see Jana and Kathy. Maybe we'll get to swing again later."

He marveled at her patience with his niece. And loved her for it. She would be a perfect mother. Probably had been a perfect mother. He frowned at the thought as it twisted through his mind. He couldn't hold on to the past and let it color his and Amanda's life now. They needed to look toward the future.

He watched Amanda bribe Kara with a cookie from their lunch, and a welcome quiet descended on the park. He shared a smile with her and held the door while she buckled his niece into the truck.

"Thanks, Mandy." He resisted the urge to pull her into his arms and squeezed her shoulders instead. "I'd have been pushing that swing all night or until the police came after me for kidnapping my own niece."

She laughed and climbed into his truck. "Not so. You'll soon figure out when to be tough and when to give in. Just like every relationship, there's a give-and-take."

"Hmm. Maybe so." He went to the driver's side with her words running through his mind. How could he convince her to give up the past so they could take hold of their future?

ten

Amanda spent most of the following week at Chad's going through things. She worked first in the master bedroom, sorting clothing and filling large trash bags for Chad to donate. He spent most of his time outdoors mowing and doing yard work, getting ready for the barn raising. She folded the last shirt and added it to the bag of men's clothing when she heard Chad come inside.

"Mandy, where are you?" His voice preceded him down the hall.

"In the bedroom."

He stepped through the doorway and watched her tie the bag closed then turned toward the pile of bags leaning against the wall beside the door. Raw emotions of pain and anger ran across his face, but when he turned back to her a smile lifted the corner of his mouth. "You've been busy."

"Yes, and I've made a mess in here." She tugged the bag toward the others. "We need to get these out of the house because today's Thursday. What time is the social worker coming?"

"Can you believe I almost forgot her?" Chad looked at his watch. "We've still got a couple of hours. I'll load these in the back of my truck and deliver them after she leaves. Maybe she'll know a good place to take them."

"Good idea. I'll help." Amanda pulled a bag upright and started to lift it when Chad stopped her.

"Last time I checked, I'm still the boss here." He picked up a bag and grinned around it at her. "Leave that alone and follow me. I have a better job for you."

In the living room, he stopped and motioned with his head toward the dining room. "Why don't you fix us some sandwiches?"

"Yes, sir." Amanda saluted and marched to the tune of his laughter through the dining room toward the kitchen. She turned back to see him heading out the door with the stuffed bag.

After they ate, Chad helped Amanda clean up their mess. She turned from the refrigerator and bumped into his chest when he threw the empty potato chip bag in the trash. Her heart picked up speed and warmth crept toward her face as they faced each other, neither moving away.

She finally spoke. "I found something in the bedroom that I'd like to show you." Like a coward, she turned and ran from the room. "Find a chair somewhere. I'll be right back."

In the bedroom, she picked up Jessica's Bible and held it close to her heart. *Lord, help me. Being this close to Chad day after day is so hard, but I feel like it's the right thing to do. If I shouldn't be here, show me. Above all help me trust You for the strength to do Your will.*

When she'd first started helping Chad, she'd done it for Jessica and for Kara because she thought Chad had betrayed her. Now she knew he was a victim of Susan's lies just as she had been. She thought her love for him had died, but it hadn't. If anything, she loved him more now that she knew what he'd gone through because of Susan and his own mistakes.

She hurried back to the kitchen with what she considered a treasure and hoped he would, too.

❧

Chad's heart pounded from being so close to Amanda. He shook off his desire to declare his love for her and sank into the first chair he came to in the dining room. She wasn't ready to erase the past and might never be, but he couldn't give up on them yet. He needed her for Kara, but even more, he needed her for himself. He looked up as she walked through the wide doorway from the living room with a smile on her face and a book clutched in her arms.

He grinned. "What've you got there?"

She sat down across the corner of the table from him and placed the book on the table. A Bible. He raised an eyebrow, waiting for her explanation.

"I think this is something Kara will want to keep." Her slender hand stroked the cover before she opened it. "Look here in Psalms. See how Jessica has highlighted certain verses and underlined others? There are notes in the margins, too. Some are prayers."

She turned toward the back of the Bible. "Look at this one in Ephesians 4:18. 'Having the understanding darkened, being alienated from the life of God through the ignorance that is in them, because of the blindness of their heart.' She highlighted that and wrote beside it a sort of prayer. It says, 'Illuminate the hearts, Lord Jesus, of those who do not know they need You.'"

Amanda looked up at him, her eyes like sparkling emeralds. He couldn't turn away even though something inside clenched at her words. "This is a testimony of Jessica's relationship with the Lord, Chad. I knew she was a Christian, but this Bible is like her voice has remained to lead others to Him. When Kara is older she can read through the verses that meant so much to her mother and also read the comments and prayers that Jessica left. Surely they will bring her so much peace to know her parents are in heaven watching for her to also come home."

Chad didn't know what to say. He'd rather not think about Jessica. Being in her house without her was hard enough. Amanda thrust the Bible at him. "Here, why don't you hold on to this for Kara. Keep it until she's old enough to read her mother's thoughts. Maybe you'd like to read them, too, but I really think Kara needs this."

He gave a quick nod as he took the Bible. "Sure, I'll see that she gets it when the time's right. Thanks, Mandy."

He didn't know what he'd said wrong, but her eyes dimmed. She stood and looked around. "I think the house is as clean as it gets. I'd better get out of here before the social worker shows up. Do you want me to keep going through things tomorrow?"

"Yeah, if you don't mind." Chad stood, too, leaving the Bible on the table.

Her smile made him wish the social worker wasn't coming. Having Amanda here helped him forget that Jessica wasn't and never would be again. He walked her to the door and let her go out ahead of him. "How's your new car doing?"

She flashed a smile over her shoulder. "I love it. I can't even hear the motor when it's running. Thanks for helping me get a good one."

He chuckled. "No problem, only you already had it picked out, remember. All I did was ride with you and say it looked fine." He opened her door and she got in. "Hey, Amanda, be careful driving home. I'll see you tomorrow."

"Okay." Her smile and wave stayed with him as he watched her back out and turn onto the road in front.

Amanda's car disappeared from sight as another car turned in and stopped. The social worker. Not looking forward to having his house inspected, but glad to get the requirement over, he waited to greet her.

❧

As soon as the social worker left, Chad returned to the house and stood for a moment staring at the living room without seeing it. He sank to the couch and leaned back, still unsure how he felt. Mandy. He had to call her. He'd never make it through the next few days without her. He pulled his cell phone from his pocket and punched the buttons that connected him to the one person he knew he could count on.

The sound of her voice helped him breathe. "Mandy, thank you."

"For what?"

He laughed. "A million reasons. Answering your phone. Talking to me when you should be running away as fast as you can. Working here, helping get this place ready for Kara." His voice dropped. "Just being you."

"Chad, what's wrong?" Amanda's voice sharpened. "Did the social worker come? I passed a car with a woman in it. I thought that might be her."

"Yeah, it was. She just left. Kara comes home Monday morning early. I want you with me, Mandy. Please?"

"That's wonderful, Chad." Amanda laughed. "You had me thinking something had gone wrong. Of course, I'll go with you. What about Sunday? Do you have your usual visit?"

He ran his fingers through his hair, glad she couldn't see him. "Yeah, Sunday afternoon. Can you come?"

Her laughter brought a smile to his lips, and he relaxed a little more and wished he wasn't so scared. Mandy didn't seem to be. Of course, Kara didn't scream every time she looked at her, either.

"Sure, Chad. I'll help you out on one condition. You have to come to my folks' for dinner after church Sunday. You do plan to attend Sunday morning, don't you?" Her voice carried a lilt as if she had the upper hand.

He grinned. "So, you think your folks will appreciate your conditions?"

"I think so." She sighed. "Mom's been after me to invite you, and Brad can't wait to see you again. My dad says he's fine with it. As long as he gets to eat, he doesn't care who sits across the table from him. Looks like you have no choice unless you want to face your sweet, little niece all by yourself."

He chuckled. "Got me over a barrel, huh? Okay, count me in. And thanks, Mandy. I'll see you in the morning."

As they hung up, Chad leaned back, amazed at how relaxed he felt after talking to her. With Amanda beside him, he could face Kara without fear.

❧

Sunday after church Amanda rode to the house with Chad. She remained quiet, as if she sensed his concern, and he didn't feel like talking, either. Even with her assurance that her family wanted him there, he had a hard time believing they really did. She said she'd told them Chad's story about Susan, and her dad only shook his head. But her mom sympathized with Chad, saying Susan needed prayer, for surely she would reap what she sowed. Brad's reaction warmed Chad's heart. Amanda said he'd grinned and said, "Didn't I tell you so, and it was even worse than I figured."

Now Chad held Amanda's hand as they crossed the yard from the driveway. Everyone else was already there. She stopped at the door and gave his hand a squeeze. "They don't blame you, Chad. Even if they had, they would have forgiven you."

His eyebrows lifted as he searched her face. "Are you saying you've forgiven me?"

She hesitated, and then looked into his eyes. "Yes, and it was easy because there isn't that much to forgive. You were a victim same as me. The hurt may take longer to heal, though."

"I see." He opened the door, unwilling to go into the issue at the moment. "We'd better go inside before they come get us."

As soon as they stepped inside, Brad called out. "Hey, long time no see, buddy."

Chad grinned at his old friend. After a handshake and a round of shoulder slapping, he felt as if he'd come home.

☙

Amanda slipped past them, shared a smile with her dad, and went into the kitchen. Her mother poked a long-handled fork into something in a large Crock-Pot on the counter. She put the lid back on and turned toward Amanda with a smile. "Did you get him here finally?"

"Yes." She grinned and shook her head. "I had to bargain with him, though."

Esther stopped at the door with a stack of dishes in her arms. "Now you've got my curiosity. What kind of bargain?"

Amanda laughed. "He doesn't know it, but I'd have gone with him to get Kara tomorrow anyway. He'd have a hard time keeping me away. And before you say anything—" She held a hand up to her mother who started to speak.

"I know you think I'll get hurt. We've already gone over that, and I understand the risks of loving and losing a child, not to mention getting hurt by Chad all over again. I won't deny it's a possibility, but it'll be fine. I promise I won't wear my emotions on my sleeve. At least I have a job that pays my way until school starts."

"I'm your mother, Amanda." Brenda Davis sniffed. "I have a right to be concerned about my children. Only I'm concerned about Chad, too. And that baby. What if they get too attached to you?"

Amanda sighed. "I'll be busy with school in another six weeks. Chad has to go back to Rockford to get ready for his classes and get Kara settled before school starts, too. We know what future we had was destroyed by our past." She looked from her mother to Esther, who still waited at the door. "Give us some credit for being smart enough to let dead dogs lie. We're friends, that's all."

Esther gave her a smile that could've meant anything and went through the door into the dining room. Her mother turned back to the stove and picked up some pot holders.

"The roast is done. Would you mind mashing potatoes while I take this up?"

"Sure." Amanda helped get the food on the table and then called the men in from the living room while Esther went out the back door to find her children.

They had just sat down when they heard the front door open and Karen's voice. "Mom, Dad, are we too late?"

Dad chuckled and answered as his oldest daughter appeared in the dining room doorway surrounded by her family. "That depends. We haven't eaten up the food if that's what you mean."

"Oh good. We're starved." Wayne stepped past his wife. "Are the extra chairs still in the closet?"

"Yep, help yourself." Dad winked at Mom. "Think we might need a bigger table."

"Oh no." She shook her head. "We'll scoot a little closer together and make room. More cozy this way. One of you girls, come here with your chair. I've got room beside me and Grandpa's got room at his end."

She moved to one side and eleven-year-old Treva set a folding chair in place between her grandmother and her cousin, Ellie. Amanda watched her nieces fit in beside their grandparents. She moved her chair closer to Chad's and pulled her seven-year-old nephew's chair toward hers to make room for Karen on the other side while Wayne found room across the table. Sawyer looked from one end of the table to the other and said, "How come I'm the only boy in this family?"

Everyone laughed as his dad answered, "Now you know how I felt growing up with two sisters."

Amanda shared a smile with her sister as their dad held a hand out to either side and said, "Let's pray."

Chad reached for her right hand and she took Sawyer's with her left. She tried to concentrate on the feel of her nephew's small smooth fingers rather than the warm sensation of being surrounded and protected by Chad's strong, capable hand. She scarcely heard her dad's prayer blessing the food. Chad uncurled his fingers from hers first, leaving heat in her face that she hoped didn't show.

After the rush of filling their plates subsided, Mom asked her son-in-law, "Wayne, have you met Chad Randall?"

Wayne met Chad's gaze and shook his head. "No, I don't believe so."

"Oh that's right," Amanda said. "You guys got married after—"

Her gaze flew to Chad's. He smiled and finished her sentence, "After we broke up." He looked across the table to explain. "Amanda and I dated through high school and while we were in college. We met again this summer, and she's been graciously helping me out of an impossible situation. I don't know what I'd do without her."

Wayne nodded. "Karen's told me about the damage from the tornadoes. I'm sorry about your family. That's got to be hard."

"Yeah, it is. Thanks." Chad didn't say more and the conversation drifted to other topics.

By the time their dessert plates held only crumbs of apple pie, Amanda was ready to go see Kara. Chad had entered into the discussion of her dad's favorite football players and teams, and seemed in no hurry to leave.

"There's a game on now if you'd like to relax and watch it." Amanda's dad pushed back from the table and stood.

Wayne followed his lead. "Sounds like a good idea to me. Brad, Chad, you guys coming, too?"

"Sure." Brad stood.

Amanda knew if she didn't do something quick, she'd lose Chad to the world of Sunday afternoon sports, and he'd miss an important time of bonding with his niece. She grabbed his arm as he stood. "No way. Chad can't join you because he has a date with a beautiful little girl."

Brad grinned. "Really, Amanda. We aren't overly humble, are we?"

"Not me, you goofus." Amanda laughed at her older brother. "I'm the chaperone. Kara is his date and she is beautiful, believe me. She's also not quite a year old and she wouldn't understand being stood up, so we've got to get going."

As she talked, she tugged Chad away from the table. He laughed and went willingly. "Mr. Davis, thanks for the invitation, but looks like I've got to go."

"Maybe another time. There'll be another game next Sunday. Glad to have you." Amanda's dad left no doubt that he had forgiven Chad for any hurt from the past. Amanda hoped Chad got the message.

"Thank you, sir." Chad smiled and turned to Amanda's mom. "Mrs. Davis, I haven't eaten so well for a long time. Thank you."

"You are certainly welcome."

Amanda tugged on his arm. "Come on, Chad, we've got to go. Kara wants to play on the swings again."

He nodded and looked from one adult to another as they stood waiting. "Now that we've got the house ready, my niece is being released into my custody. I'm getting legal guardianship, but if all goes well, I hope to one day adopt her. I'm the only family she has."

Mom's eyes were suspiciously moist. Amanda half expected her to grab Chad in a motherly hug, but she didn't. Karen, however, had no such reservations. She pushed past Amanda and squeezed Chad to his obvious surprise, although he gave her a couple of awkward pats on the back.

She pulled back and grinned from Chad to Amanda and back. "You've got my support, Chad. If you need anything, just let us know. And if that little girl needs more family, you know where to find us."

"That's right." Esther agreed, and Brad's grin spread across his face, although he didn't speak.

As Wayne and her parents added their support, Amanda looked up and saw raw emotion on Chad's face. She whispered so only he could hear, "Didn't I tell you?"

He shook his head and blinked. "I don't know what to say. Mandy told me you believe in forgiving. Now I know why she's such a wonderful person. She has to be coming from a family like this. Thank you all. Kara couldn't find a family any better to influence her life for good than this one."

As they said their good-byes and headed out the door, Amanda's heart sang. Sharing Kara with her family sounded like an excellent idea. If only the sharing could be permanent.

eleven

On Monday morning Amanda's excitement moved through her emotions like a bubbling stream. She stood beside Chad as he turned the old-fashioned door ringer that would bring Kara to them.

Kathy let them in. Her smile seemed dimmer than usual. "She's in the family room playing with some toys."

After they entered the family room, Kathy's daughters slipped out without speaking. Kathy watched them go then turned back and shook her head. "They've been moping around all morning. We may have to stop taking babies if this keeps up. They get so attached to the little ones. We all do, but this girl's been special."

Amanda sank to the floor beside Kara, who hadn't noticed them yet. "Hey, sweetheart."

Kara looked up with a surprised expression before her arms waved and she squealed. She flopped forward on hands and knees and crawled the short distance to Amanda, then grabbing fists full of Amanda's clothing pulled herself to a standing position. Amanda laughed and squeezed her tight.

"Are you ready to go home, precious?" Amanda looked up at Chad who still stood just inside the room watching as if he were afraid to venture closer. "Come on, Chad, Kara's glad to see us."

"I see that." He turned to Kathy. "Does she have any belongings?"

Kathy motioned toward the couch. "There are a few clothes and toys in the bags there."

"A few? Three bags full." Amanda laughed and stood with

Kara in her arms. "That seems like a lot for such a little person."

"I know." Kathy smiled. "The girls and I get carried away sometimes." She patted Kara's back as she walked past. "Like I said, this one has been special. She's been loved and it shows. The behavior of even the babies tells a lot about their background. I don't mind letting her go home because I know you'll love her. Can you get all of that?"

Chad lifted the two large trash bags and swung them around to rest against his shoulders. "I can come back for the smaller one and the diaper bag."

"I'll carry those." Kathy slung the diaper bag over her shoulder and picked up the smaller plastic bag. "We may as well make one trip."

On the way to the truck, Amanda decided she needed to have a serious talk with Chad. What could be sweeter than the feel of Kara in her arms? If she could, she'd gladly hold her on her lap all the way home, but Chad hadn't even touched his niece yet. If he didn't get over his fear of her, how could he provide the security she needed?

Kara smiled and babbled in her own baby language as they went down the walk to the street. Amanda let Kathy hold Kara and set her in the car seat. Kathy kissed the baby's cheek, told her bye, and then backed out and closed the door.

She swiped at her eyes as Chad set the bags in the back of the truck. "I'll miss her."

Amanda shook her head. "I couldn't be a foster parent, but I admire those of you who do."

Kathy shrugged and laughed. "They aren't all like Kara. Sometimes when they leave, I'm ready for the break. With all of them, I pray I've made a difference in their lives for the better."

"I'm sure you do." Amanda climbed in the truck. "Thank you for being here for Kara. We appreciate your loving care of her. You and your girls."

"You're welcome." Kathy stepped back and lifted her hand in farewell. "May God go with you and Kara."

She turned and walked back to the house.

꙳

Chad didn't speak on the drive to the farm, and Amanda decided her talk could wait until a better time. When he pulled in beside her car and stopped, he turned to her. "Would you mind staying this afternoon to make sure she's settled in? If she recognizes the house, it might upset her."

Amanda nodded. "I know. I wondered about that, too. If you need me, I'll stay. I still have some closets to go through."

"There's plenty of time for that." He looked out the windshield. "I thought I'd run into town and pick up some groceries. What do babies eat, anyway?"

"Maybe you should stay with her and let me go to town." Amanda smiled at the startled look Chad turned her way.

Kara let out a squeal at the same time. He jerked and twisted to see her. "Is she all right?"

Amanda laughed. "She's fine, just getting tired of us sitting here. She wants to get out and see where we are."

"Oh." Chad opened his door and slid out.

He came around to help Amanda, but she already had her door open. He held it while she jumped to the ground. She waited until he opened the back door of the cab and shook her head when he stepped back to let her tend to Kara.

"You'll get used to her, Chad. She isn't as fragile as you think." She lifted the strap and pulled Kara from the seat. "In fact, she's a sturdy little girl who's going to wrap you around her little finger before you know what's happened. Isn't that right, precious?"

Kara babbled her answer and clapped her hands as Amanda settled her on her arm. Amanda laughed, losing her heart all over again to the little girl. She couldn't resist a sweet hug and kiss on the smooth little cheek that entered her heart as balm. If any child could fill the emptiness of her arms and her heart, this one could. Only she couldn't keep Kara. She wasn't hers to hold for more than a few minutes at a time, and as Chad became used to his niece those minutes would fade into nothing.

Chad lifted a bag from the back. Amanda reached in and pulled the diaper bag from the backseat. She sighed. He wasn't ready to bond yet, but he would be tonight after she went home. He'd have to. Kara might sleep through the night, but if she went to sleep early, she'd more than likely be awake just as early.

Inside the house, Chad stood in the middle of the living room floor. "I should probably put this in her room, don't you think?"

She nodded. "Chad, are you still sleeping on the sofa in here?"

"Yeah, why?" He gave her a puzzled look.

"Because I assume you intend for Kara to sleep in her bedroom and that's quite a distance away. Why don't you sleep in one of the other bedrooms? The master bedroom would be closer to her, so you could hear her since it's just across the hall."

An emotional mix of fear and pain shadowed his eyes as he stared at her in silence. Finally he shook his head. "I can't do that. Maybe the spare room. Don't they have intercom-type things for babies?"

"Baby monitors? Sure. I haven't seen one here, though."

"I'll buy one. Where do I find them?" He looked so helpless, standing with the bag of Kara's clothes resting on his shoulder as if he might bolt at any moment.

If she could take his pain and fear and bear them for him, she would. He had to work through the grief just as she'd had to when Jeff and Charity died. And he had to get over his fear of Kara by taking as much responsibility for her as possible. She'd help him today, but he'd have to start taking over so he could gain the confidence he needed to parent his niece. Before long he'd be going back to Rockford where he'd become a single parent, and that thought settled as a heavy weight on Amanda's heart.

"Let me make you a list. If you'd like to grab lunch in town, I'll fix for Kara and me here." She laughed at the relieved look on his face and would've teased him about running out on her, but figured he wouldn't appreciate her joke since that was exactly what he was doing.

After Chad left, Amanda took Kara into the kitchen and set her in the highchair with a cracker for each hand. "You chew on that while I look for something to go with it."

The pantry revealed several boxes of macaroni and cheese. A further look into the canned goods and Amanda had tuna and peas. That should be easy to fix.

She backed out of the small space and smiled at Kara. "Hey, no one ever said I was the best cook in the land, did they?"

Kara gave her a wide smile smeared with wet cracker and squealed her agreement. She looked so adorable. Amanda laughed. "Hang in there. This shouldn't take long."

Fifteen minutes later, cheesy sauce joined the wet cracker on Kara's face. As her tummy filled, her eyes drooped. Amanda cleaned her little charge and took her to the rocking chair in her bedroom. They settled into a regular rhythm while the warm, sweet weight of Chad's child found a home in Amanda's heart.

Within minutes Kara slept, but Amanda didn't stop rocking. For the first time in five years, she felt almost whole. She kept a steady movement, her arms relishing the soft burden until one tear slid down her cheek. Another followed. She couldn't do this. She stood and gently deposited the baby in her bed before slipping from the room.

Silent tears continued to fall as she hurried down the hall into the living room and curled up on the sofa. This shouldn't be happening. She wiped the tears that wouldn't stop and still they came. It was no use. She'd cried after Charity died until she thought she had no tears left, but now she didn't know why she cried.

Chad and Kara were far too important to her. She'd never stopped loving Chad through all the years while her heart was broken. He hadn't loved her enough, but she'd loved him too much. Only that wasn't true.

Susan had stolen from both of them. She'd taken their love and left them hurt and empty. Then she'd grabbed the remains for herself, but to what end? How could she possibly be happy after what she'd done?

"Oh, Susan, why'd you do such a thing?" Amanda's whisper remained unanswered, because there was no answer that made sense. Sin had many excuses, but never a good reason.

She wept and prayed, *Lord, I don't understand why Charity and Jessica had to die, but I trust You. I know they're with You now and that's wonderful. I was spared. Kara escaped injury. Your Word tells us all things work together for good to them that love God. I love You, Lord. I don't think I've ever stopped loving Chad, but I don't know why we've been thrown together this way. Help me to trust You completely.*

After a while Amanda dried her tears and rose from the sofa. The kitchen needed cleaning after their lunch and Chad would be getting home soon.

Only he didn't come home when she expected. She had the kitchen spotless and had rummaged through the drawers, sorting and trying to decide what Chad might need and what should be put in storage. She taped a second box shut when she heard the crunch of tires in the drive outside. Fighting the urge to run and welcome Chad home, she stayed in the kitchen to finish her job.

The front door opened and closed. Amanda watched from the kitchen until Chad stepped into the dining room and set several plastic bags on the table. She couldn't stay back any longer. "What did you do, buy out the stores? No wonder you were gone so long."

She lifted a gallon of milk out of doubled bags. "Oh good. We used the last of the milk for lunch."

"I knew it was getting low." He turned toward the door. "I'll get the rest."

"There's more?" Amanda watched him walk away without answering. She turned to the remaining bags, curious to see what he'd bought. Most of the items from her list were there as well as several canned goods and bags of frozen vegetables.

He carried in a ten-pound bag of red potatoes and another grocery bag of fresh vegetables and fruit. Amanda pulled out a cluster of bananas. "Mmm. Kara will love these."

"Good. I was hoping they'd be soft enough for her."

"Plenty."

"Is she sleeping?" He looked toward the door as if expecting her to walk in.

Amanda nodded. "Actually, I've been thinking about waking her up. Unless you'd like to stay up half the night with her tonight."

His eyes widened. "I don't think so."

When she started away, he stopped her. "Mandy, before you get her, will you promise to help us through dinner?"

She grinned. "Oh Chad. You make it sound like you're facing torture."

"Please?"

"All right." She sighed, fighting the urge to offer the perfect solution. Marriage. She shook her head as she headed down the hall toward the bedrooms. Until she knew Chad's spiritual condition, she couldn't even think of marrying him. "Be ye not unequally yoked with unbelievers" meant just that. She'd known too many who'd tried the unequal route and failed. Had Chad been a Christian before when they'd almost married? He'd gone to church with her, but she couldn't remember talking about spiritual things. She'd been so in love, she hadn't cared about anything except being with Chad. Now she knew two-way love wasn't enough. Their love must be three-way with Christ in the center. For a three-fold cord is not easily broken.

Amanda carried a wide-eyed baby back to the kitchen. "Did you get that baby monitor?"

Chad looked up from the stove where he'd started browning ground beef and nodded. "Yeah, it's in one of the bags. Why?"

Amanda lifted Kara above her head and smiled at the giggling baby. "Because this little wide-eyed girl was sitting in her bed playing with her toys. She wasn't sleeping at all."

When she lowered Kara, she almost bumped into Chad. He stood with his hands out to either side of Kara. She moved back. "What are you doing?"

"Just don't drop her."

She laughed until she noticed the white line around his lips. Her arms tightened around Kara. "Chad, it's fine. I'm not going to drop her. She's fine."

He stepped back to the stove and stirred the sizzling meat. "I don't know if I can do this, Amanda. She scares me. It's more than her crying when I try to hold her. I'm honestly scared I'll do something to hurt her."

"I doubt that." Amanda buckled Kara in her high chair. "You know why?"

"No, why?" He pulled a cookie sheet of Tater Tots from the oven and set them on the stove top.

"Because you'll handle her with kid gloves. In fact, she'll be craving excitement so much, she'll probably become a terrible tomboy."

He gave her a sharp look.

"I'm kidding, Chad. You'll do fine." She crossed to the stove. "What are you fixing?"

"Tater Tot casserole. Jessica showed me how to make it. This is her recipe." He grinned, appearing relaxed for the first time since Kara appeared in the room. "You'll like it. Even a baby with only four teeth should be able to eat it. She can, can't she?"

"Depends on what else you put in it."

Chad shrugged. "Not much. Cheese, mushroom soup, and milk."

Amanda laughed. "Yes, she'll gum it if she doesn't have enough teeth. Don't worry." She pointed at the hamburger. "At least you didn't grill steaks."

Before she knew what was coming, Chad leaned over and left a kiss on her forehead. "Thanks, Mandy."

He grinned at her shocked look and winked. "Next time I won't miss."

She didn't want to think too much on his meaning, so she hid behind Kara's squeal and grabbed a sippy cup for her.

twelve

Amanda patted her middle and pushed away from the table. "I didn't know you could cook, Chad. That was good."

He chuckled. "If you want to eat Tater Tot casserole or chili all the time, I guess I can cook. That's about the extent of my culinary talents."

"Hmm, does that mean you're planning chili for tomorrow night?" Amanda took Kara from the high chair.

"Maybe. Are you staying if I do?" Chad scooted his chair back as she headed toward the door with his niece.

Amanda gave him a smile. "Something tells me you're trying to weasel out of spending time alone with this sweet angel. We are going to visit a washcloth in the bathroom, and then I need to head home."

Chad didn't respond so Amanda washed Kara's face and hands then set her with some toys on the living room carpet while she helped Chad by cleaning the dining room table.

Several minutes later, Kara crawled toward Amanda, crying when she tried to leave. She opened the door but couldn't step outside with the heart-wrenching wails following her. "Chad, I need help here."

He shrugged. "Maybe she's sleepy."

"Try picking her up. Pat her back." Amanda fought the urge to reach for the baby. Much more and she'd be crying, too. "Turn her away from me. If you distract her, she'll be fine. Mostly, just love her. You have to take care of her tonight, Chad. Remember what I've told you and you'll be fine. If you forget something, I'm only a phone call away."

He caught Kara just before she reached Amanda. The

crying stopped, but her hands stretched toward Amanda while she said, "Manmaa."

"Oh Chad." Tears burned Amanda's eyes while she longed to gather the little girl close. "I can't do this. She's so precious."

"Why don't we get married, Mandy?" Chad drew her attention to him. "It makes sense. The love is still there for me, and I think for you, too."

A tear rolled down her cheek. She caught Kara to her and held her as if she were a shield against Chad's love. She whispered, "But love isn't enough."

"Are you saying you do love me?" He lifted Kara's hand and rubbed his thumb against the back of it. "Or is your love only for her?"

Kara laid her head on Amanda's shoulder as if she didn't want to leave her safe haven, but she didn't pull her hand from Chad's. He spoke quietly. "Mandy, please answer me."

Her eyes met his and held. What could she say that he would understand and accept? Could she tell him that God had been impressing upon her the importance of being equally yoked with a believer? He'd think she hadn't forgiven him for what Susan did. He'd take offense if she implied he wasn't a Christian.

"I love you both, but marriage for the wrong reasons would be a mistake. I can't do that." She started toward the back of the house. "I think you're right about Kara being sleepy. It's early, but I'll get her ready for bed, and then I need to go home. Can you please bring a fresh bottle for her?"

Chad's hand dropped as Amanda moved away. She felt his gaze until she entered Kara's bedroom. He didn't follow her and she was glad. He didn't know how close to giving in to his suggestion of marriage she had come. But if this was God's second chance for them, He would have to let her know without doubt. Right now she didn't understand why she and Chad had been thrown back together, but she didn't think marriage was the answer. As much as she wished.

She grabbed the things she needed for Kara's bath then afterward carried her back to the bedroom in a large fluffy towel. Bath time had always been one of her pleasures of motherhood. Charity had always smelled so sweet and became especially cuddly after a bath while she rocked her to sleep. Kara was no different. They settled into the rocking chair with the bottle Chad had left in easy reach, and within minutes, the baby's eyes drifted closed. When Amanda knew she was truly asleep, she set the bottle aside and settled her in her bed with a kiss. She tugged the quilt in place and went back to the living room.

Chad stood when she entered. "Is she asleep?"

Amanda nodded and handed him the empty bottle, not sure of her voice.

"If I offended you, I'm sorry." Chad set the bottle on the table and followed her outside. The sun had moved beyond the western horizon, but its light still lingered.

She turned and smiled at him. "No, you honored me by your offer. I just think we should remain friends for now. So much happened to us that I didn't even know until you told me. I want to help you with Kara. You need to take care of her. I apologize for taking over just now. I wasn't thinking."

He frowned. "What do you mean?"

"Putting her to bed. That's an excellent time for you to bond with her." She reached her car and turned to face him. "Take her from her bed as soon as she wakes in the morning. Be cheerful and don't let her know she scares you. You'll soon have her going to you first before anyone else."

A quick laugh tore from Chad. "I doubt that. She hates me now so..."

He didn't finish his sentence, but Amanda understood his concern. She touched his hand. "It won't take long, Chad.

Babies have short memories, and she'll forget quickly enough that you were once scared of her when you start acting confident around her."

"I'm not afraid of her." He growled the words.

She suppressed the urge to laugh. "Of course not, but sometimes the weak can be just as frightening as the strong. Especially when we care, and I know you love Kara."

He nodded. "What time will you be here tomorrow?"

"Probably not before eight, but I'll come as soon as I can." She touched his arm. "You'll be fine. Just remember, she doesn't break that easily and a few tears won't hurt her. Let her know you love her. That's all she wants."

He took a step toward her. She didn't have to guess what he wanted. Her breath caught in her throat as he touched her arms and drew her closer. His head lowered and she forgot to breathe as their lips touched.

❧

Amanda arrived at the farm Tuesday morning to the sound of Kara crying. Not bothering to knock, she rushed to the kitchen where she found Chad walking the floor with the unhappy baby.

"What's wrong?" No blood poured from any cut or scrape she could see. She touched the back of Kara's head to check for a bump.

Kara's wails changed to, "Manmaa."

As she reached toward Amanda, Chad said, "She isn't hurt. She hates me is all."

"Oh that's ridiculous."

At that moment, Kara leaned and Chad thrust her toward Amanda. She caught the little girl in her arms and brought her close.

"You love Uncle Chad, don't you?"

Kara's answer was a hiccupping sob as she laid her head against Amanda's neck.

In the silence, Chad smirked, his eyebrows lifted as if he knew best. "What'd I say? Look at her, Mandy. I tried. I got her out of bed and changed her diaper. She cried through the whole ordeal, so I brought her in here thinking she might be hungry." He waved a hand at an untouched bowl of oatmeal on her high chair tray. "I couldn't even get her in that thing. She kept arching her back and screaming. I think she was calling for you. But I can't tell if it's Momma or Manda."

Amanda patted Kara's back. If this weren't so serious, she'd laugh. But something had to be done. Chad couldn't parent Kara if she wouldn't let him. What could they do?

"I've had it." He started toward the door. "The barn raising is Saturday. I've got work to do outside."

"Wait." Amanda grabbed his arm. "Let's eat breakfast together. I'm hungry and I assume you haven't eaten yet either."

He hesitated, eyed the oatmeal he'd left on the counter, and shrugged with a sigh. "All right."

"Can you help me get Kara in her chair?" Amanda stood in front of the high chair and tried to look helpless. "Pull the tray out, please."

She set his niece in the chair and backed away. "Thanks. I'll get the oatmeal while you snap her into place."

When no tears erupted, Amanda congratulated herself. Then reality hit. Kara would still be crying if she wasn't there. She had to help them come together and depend on each other, because soon Chad would take Kara to Rockford and they'd have to get along without her. She'd have to get along without them. Unexpected emotion blocked her throat.

To hide her feelings and keep tears from forming, Amanda busied herself with the oatmeal. She dropped bread in the toaster and got margarine and jelly from the refrigerator then filled two glasses with milk.

Chad pulled a chair up to the high chair and held the

spoon of oatmeal up to Kara's mouth. Amanda held her breath when Kara let him feed her. Chad's eyes met hers and his eyebrows lifted, but he didn't speak and neither did she.

After they ate breakfast, Amanda took Kara outdoors to watch Chad finish mowing around the barn foundation. She and Kara sat on the back deck where they'd be a safe distance from the mower and the loud noise it made, but where they could see. Amanda held Kara's hands and "walked" around the deck several times before Amanda grew tired. After they sat in a lounge chair and played patty-cake and peekaboo, Amanda stood with Kara and pointed toward Chad.

"Look at Uncle Chad, sweetie pie. See how he's working to fix your home?" She kissed the baby's cheek. "Uncle Chad loves you. He's a little scared of you because he's a big, strong man and you're a little, tiny girl. That just means he's afraid he'll hurt you, not that he really will. I want you to stop crying when you're with Uncle Chad. Can you do that?"

Kara turned from watching the mower to look into Amanda's face with a serious expression. Amanda wondered how much an eleven-month-old child could understand. All at once Kara squealed and waved her arms, laughing as if in agreement. Then she said, "Manmaa."

Amanda held the sweet child tight and wished she had the right to be called Momma. She turned away from the railing. Kara might be calling for Jessica, or she might be saying Amanda, but she certainly wasn't calling her Momma. She might as well accept that fact. There was no reason she would.

After a while Amanda lowered Kara into her playpen. Shade from the house and a gentle breeze kept them cool. A couple of toys, including a favorite homemade rag doll, occupied Kara's attention until her eyelids lowered and she went to sleep. Amanda covered her with a thin sheet as a barrier to insects and picked up the rag doll. The cloth doll, dressed in an old-fashioned pinafore dress, had bright blue eyes embroidered on its smiling face. Someone had spent a lot of time on Kara's doll. Probably Jessica. She'd always liked to sew. The stack of quilts in her closet testified to that as did several tiny dresses with smocking and embroidery that must have been done by hand. A sharp pang of loss hit Amanda. She laid the doll back in the playpen beside Kara.

Whether her talk with Kara made a difference, or Chad's breakfast feeding success Tuesday morning encouraged him, Amanda didn't know. Throughout the week she insisted he bathe the little one and put her to bed. After that first time, she saw a difference in Chad first and Kara second. He became more confident as he held and played with his niece. By Friday he no longer held her as if he might let go of her any second. Instead he wrapped his arms around her, squeezing and nuzzling her soft neck to her delight.

Amanda stood at the door while Chad kissed Kara good night and tucked her into bed. He turned with a smile. "Your turn."

She hesitated. She shouldn't have a turn. She didn't belong. No matter how much she loved them, they weren't hers to love. Only she did. Deeply.

She crossed the room to the crib and looked down at Kara. Chad slipped his arm around her waist. *Father, thank You for the love I had with Jeff and Charity. And thank You for Chad and Kara. I know they aren't mine to love, but I do love them. With all my heart.* She bent forward and placed a kiss on Kara's forehead then lifted the bed railing into place. Together she and Chad left the room.

"Tomorrow's the big day." Chad spoke as soon as they reached the living room. "Pastor Mattson said they'd be here by eight."

Amanda smiled at him. "Kind of exciting isn't it? It'll be like a trip back into the old days when people helped each other and had fun doing it."

"Yeah, a barn raising was a big event back then, but I consider it a big event now, too." He pulled her down to sit on the sofa beside him. "I love the smell of cinnamon and spices from your baking today. Makes it seem like a real home."

"You can make a real home for Kara, Chad."

His arm tightened around her shoulders, but he didn't carry the thought further. "I've got the lumber we need. I hope. Not to mention hardware and tools."

"The men will bring tools." She laughed. "And a lot of know-how. Our church is blessed with carpenters, one professional. We have a plumber and an electrician. I'd say we're pretty set."

"I guess so." As they leaned against the sofa, his arm still circled her shoulders.

She wanted to snuggle into the warmth of his side but stood instead. "I've got to get home while there's still daylight to see the way."

Chad laughed and stood, too. "Just because we're planning an activity that would fit better in the nineteenth century doesn't mean you're driving a buggy. Your car has headlights, doesn't it? Can't you stay a little longer?"

Amanda looked away from the pleading in his eyes. The longing he might see reflected in her eyes if she looked at him.

She took a step toward the door and laughed. "I've been here every day this week. Isn't that enough? You'll get tired of me soon."

"No I won't." Chad followed her to the door and caught her arm before she had it open. "I love you, Mandy. I've never stopped and I—"

"No." She swung to face him. "You can't say those things. We can't feel them. There's still too much between us."

He brushed wetness from her cheeks before she knew she was crying. "What? I see two hearts longing to beat as one. That would be us, Mandy, if you'd allow it to be. It once was that way. Remember?"

His arms enfolded her as she wept against his chest. His voice rumbled in her ear. "We had what other people envied. Maybe that's what tore us apart. Envy. Deception. But that's past now, Mandy. It's time to take back what we lost. Don't you believe in second chances?"

She nodded and looked up at him. "Of course. God has given us each a second chance. Oh Chad. That's what life is all about."

"Sure, but I'm talking about us. We need this chance to make things right. How about it?"

Why couldn't he understand he needed a chance to make his life right before God? How could she tell him without implying he wasn't good enough? If she said the wrong thing, she could easily drive him away from God. *Lord, help me.* She shook her head. "I can't, Chad. Not now. Maybe not ever. So much has happened. To you. To me."

His bitterness toward God isn't all of it. I have problems, too. Her eyes burned again with unshed tears. How could their lives ever be renewed when so much had been taken from them? How could she offer herself to Chad with the ugly scars of her infertility standing between them?

"We can work through it, Mandy. Because of all that's gone on before, we're stronger now. We can make it this time. I know we can." He held her close, but she pulled away.

"I'm sorry, Chad. I love you, but we can't be more than friends." She jerked the door open and stepped out before he stopped her again. "It's getting late. I'll see you tomorrow."

thirteen

Amanda would never forgive him. No matter what she said to the contrary, the barrier of unforgiveness stood between them. He watched her taillights disappear and locked the door. What had he done to deserve this? He'd lost Amanda because of what? Being stupid enough to believe Susan. That's what. He slammed the heel of his hand against the door frame and winced, glad for the painful distraction.

He rubbed his hand. Amanda wasn't blameless. Why'd she run off to California so quickly, anyway? And get married to the first guy she met?

He sank to the sofa and let the long-ago events that had ruined his life run through his mind. Sometimes his life seemed a total waste. For the last several years, he'd poured all his energy into being the best teacher he could. Wasn't there more to life than that?

The emptiness of his life gnawed at the center of his core causing him to jump from the sofa. He strode silently back to Kara's bedroom and stood looking down at her. She was becoming more precious to him every day, but she didn't come close to easing his restlessness. Maybe she contributed to the strange foreboding he couldn't shake. He didn't know.

He grabbed the baby monitor and clipped it to his belt. He needed to get out of the house for a while. Outside, the stars twinkled against a darkening sky. Amanda should be almost home by now. But he wouldn't think of her. He forced his mind to the barn raising set for the next day and headed toward the cement floor where the materials were stacked and waiting. It was too late, but he'd make a final check of lumber and supplies to get his mind on something besides his discontent.

≥◆

The first car pulled into Chad's driveway while he tried to dress Kara. At least she wasn't crying anymore. After a week of seeing him every day, she must have decided he wasn't a monster after all. Or maybe Amanda was right. Maybe he'd figured out Kara wouldn't break if he touched her. She still watched him with wary eyes, but she didn't arch her back and scream, trying to get away from him.

"Here, babe, let's get you ready for the big day." He found the neck of a cotton knit shirt and pulled it over her head, as a knock sounded and the front door opened.

Amanda stepped in and grinned at them. "Aren't you two ready yet? I figured as much, so I came early."

"Hey, we're doing pretty good." Chad defended himself, while his heart lurched at the sight of her. "If you hadn't come early, we wouldn't have gotten caught."

She laughed. "Maybe, but the others aren't far behind me." She sat on the sofa beside Chad and helped him guide one arm and then another through Kara's shirt. "This is cute. It looks like it has another shirt underneath, and I love pink. Why can't I ever find anything like this in my size?"

"That's the breaks." Chad grinned at her. Sitting so close with his baby niece reaching for her and saying "Manmaa" gave him a sense of family. Granted most of his feelings were wishes, but still he couldn't help thinking life had dealt him a cruel blow. This mock family scene should be real. He and Amanda should have a teenager by now. Or, at least a preteen. If not for Susan, they'd have been married well over fourteen years.

He believed they'd been given a second chance, and he planned to take advantage of it. Last night he'd tossed through the night, grabbing snatches of sleep while his thoughts dwelled on Amanda and all they'd lost. Maybe she hadn't forgiven him yet, but she would. As she said, she came from a family who believed in forgiveness.

"Has she eaten yet?" Amanda's question brought him to the present.

"Um, no. Am I supposed to feed her before I dress her?" He watched her cuddling the baby who had somehow transferred to her lap and wondered if he'd ever learn to be a decent father.

Amanda's smile set his heart pounding again. She shrugged. "There's no rule. It's just easier to keep her clean if she eats before she dresses."

"Oh." He stood and headed for the kitchen. "I'll fix some cereal. How messy can it be?"

Amanda mumbled something that sounded like, "You'd be surprised."

He ignored her and got out the baby cereal and fixed a bowl. He also found a bib and handed it to Amanda.

Kara was still eating when they heard tires crunching gravel in the driveway. Chad headed for the door. "I'd better get outside."

"Go ahead. We're fine. We'll be out as soon as the bowl's empty."

Chad opened the front door and found not one car but a whole caravan pulling into his driveway. As if directed by an unseen traffic controller, the trucks, vans, and cars angle parked to either side of the drive. His truck sat at the end, and Amanda had pulled into the yard close to the house. Their vehicles were blocked, but he didn't figure it mattered. In fact, he was glad. She'd have to stay until the last car left now.

He smiled and stepped off the porch to greet the church people he was rapidly coming to think of as friends. Pastor Mattson led the way with his hand outstretched. As they shook hands, he said, "Well, the crew's here. We've got experienced carpenters and a host of helpers. The women have brought enough food to feed everyone with plenty left over, I imagine."

"We have for sure." Mrs. Mattson stepped close to her husband. She shook Chad's hand. "Would you mind if we take over your kitchen today? Some of the ladies have brought dishes that need to be heated."

"Of course." He looked toward the house as Amanda stepped outside, Kara balanced on her hip. "Amanda can help you with that."

The pastor and his wife exchanged surprised looks. Chad expected them to ask questions about his relationship with Amanda, but one of the men called to the pastor. Women carrying covered dishes and full grocery bags brushed past, asking where they should set up dinner preparations. Chad pointed them toward Amanda, and they scurried toward her.

Brenda Davis, Amanda's mom, patted Chad's arm as she walked past. "Looks like we'll finally get that barn back up."

"Yes, finally." Chad had no sooner answered than Linda Maddox stopped beside him.

She held a casserole dish. Her head tilted to one side as she looked toward Amanda with Kara in her arms, directing the women inside. Her voice dropped to a confidential level. "She looks at home on your front porch, Chad."

"I'd like for her to be at home." He knew Linda had reservations about him. She didn't know the whole story. Maybe Amanda's folks did know. Maybe that helped them be more forgiving. "I hope before long she will be."

"Just don't hurt her." Linda frowned. "She's been through enough."

He gave a bitter laugh. "If anyone gets hurt, it will be me—again."

Linda looked into his eyes as if trying to decide what game

he was playing. After a bit she nodded. "Maybe so. Do you mind if I add you to my prayer list?"

Her question surprised him so much he took a step back. Did he mind? He'd once believed in prayer. Even now he didn't disbelieve. He just didn't know if God cared enough to answer. Maybe He did for people who were especially close to Him. Maybe Linda's prayers would rise to God's throne while his wouldn't.

He shrugged. "I can't see where it would hurt anything."

She smiled. "No, it won't hurt anything. If we believe, we might find the help we need." She stepped away. "Here comes Brad. I need to get this to the kitchen."

Chad realized that most of the men had already gathered at the barn site. A few straggling women headed toward the house. Kids of various ages ran around the house playing, and several had formed a baseball game in the roomy yard.

Amanda's brother called to him. "Hey Chad, we need your input out here."

Chad hurried to fall into step with Brad as they walked with long strides out to the barn site. "It's great to have you all here, Brad. Before this summer I would've never expected Amanda or her family to treat me with anything short of contempt. It's still hard to believe."

Brad grinned. "Don't know where you'd get that idea. No one's perfect. I always figured you got a bum deal. I met Susan a couple of times when she and Amanda were friends. Twice was enough for me."

"I should've seen what she was before I did."

Brad shrugged. "So you made a mistake. Mistakes can be corrected. Seems that God has His hand on you and Amanda. You've been spending some time together this summer. Have you thought about seeking His will?"

"Prayer?" Chad almost laughed. First Linda and now Brad had mentioned prayer, and he couldn't even remember the last time he'd prayed. He should've expected as much with church people. He shook his head. "Not really, but I guess it wouldn't hurt."

"Here's the man we need." Pastor Mattson called out with a wide smile, and Chad silently thanked him for distracting Brad. He welcomed the activity that kept them too busy to visit as they broke into groups to begin construction of his new barn.

ﾊ

Amanda lost Kara within minutes of the women invading Chad's house. After helping set casseroles, bags of various kinds of chips, meat platters, and dessert dishes on the table, she went looking for her baby. And mentally corrected herself for thinking of Kara as hers. Losing her when Chad took her to Rockford in another month would be hard enough without becoming too attached. If she hadn't already.

The women were spread out from the kitchen, through the dining room, and into the living room, visiting and preparing the noon meal. A couple of ladies stood on the deck outside, but Amanda didn't see Kara with them. She moved on to the living room. And found her.

In Brenda Davis's arms.

Amanda's mother sat in the rocker recliner with Kara on her lap. Amanda stood in the wide arched doorway between the two rooms and watched her mother squeeze the baby close and drop a kiss on her head.

"Looks like Grandma's getting acquainted." Linda's low voice behind Amanda startled her.

She turned with a frown. "I thought you wanted Chad to stay away from me."

Linda's eyebrows rose. "Did I say that?"

"I guess not exactly." Amanda shrugged. "It's more a feeling I had."

"Is he living the Christian life?"

With a dozen women visiting and moving about the three-room area, Linda's voice didn't carry beyond Amanda's hearing, but still she glanced at her mother. And smiled. Grandma, indeed. Oblivious to all but the baby on her lap, her mom played patty-cake with Kara and they both laughed.

"Kara doesn't have a grandma."

"Amanda?" Linda touched her shoulder. "What's that got to do with Chad's spiritual condition?"

Amanda blinked and turned to look at Linda. "I'm sorry. I was just thinking. Mom didn't get to see Charity much because we lived so far away, but Jeff's parents were there so she had grandparents who spoiled her terribly. Kara has never known a grandparent's love. That's a little sad, isn't it?"

"Yes, I guess so." Linda smiled at Amanda's mother. "Brenda looks like she'd be willing to fill in, though. So, why don't you answer me?"

"About Chad?" Amanda turned to look fully into Linda's eyes. "I don't know. I thought he was a Christian until"—she looked away—"until we broke up. Things that happened made me think he wasn't. Only now I don't know."

She took a deep breath. "I'm probably not making sense. It's just things aren't always what they seem and people get the wrong idea. Still, he seems different now. Bitter. And that concerns me."

"He's had a hard time," Linda said. "He just lost his sister and brother-in-law. He's become an instant father after being responsible for no one except himself for years. His mother died a couple of years ago, too. Add all that up and it isn't so surprising that he's having trouble coping."

Amanda nodded. "I understand, and maybe that's all it is. Or maybe what I thought was Christianity back when we were engaged was only him trying to please me."

Linda caught and held Amanda's gaze. "In that case, be careful. You aren't immune to him any more than he is to you. I've seen you both. The way you look at each other. I'm sure your mom would tell you the same thing."

Amanda's smile was tight as she glanced back at her mother. "Trust me, she's already made a few choice remarks without coming right out and telling me to keep away from Chad. 'Help him all you can, just don't let your heart get involved.' Yeah, right."

fourteen

Midmorning on Monday Amanda pulled into Chad's drive and admired the new barn through the windshield of her car. She still had trouble believing so much had been done in one day. Everyone who could pitched in, even her. The men and boys had worked hard on the building all day. Several of the women helped in the afternoon. But to erect a fine, strong building in a few hours seemed like a miracle to her. Of course, with Ron Kimbel's expert supervision, they'd all worked together as if they knew what they were doing. Looked like they had, too.

She smiled as she went to the house and tapped on the door. When Chad didn't answer, she tried the knob and found it unlocked. They weren't in the living room, dining room, or kitchen. Each room was as clean and neat as the women had left it two days before. With her heart pounding, she moved silently down the carpeted hall to the bedrooms.

The door to the bedroom Chad had been using stood open. A quick glance showed his bed was made and no one there. She looked in Kara's room next and stopped at the doorway. There in the rocking chair sat Chad with Kara cuddled on one arm, his sister's Bible resting on the chair arm while he read and rocked.

Amanda held her breath, afraid to move for fear the scene before her would vanish. As she watched, he closed the Bible, placed it on a table, and stood with Kara. In two steps he reached her bed, but he didn't immediately put her down. Chad leaned to kiss his sleeping niece before he gently lowered her into the crib. Amanda turned and fled back down the hall, tears filling her eyes.

They didn't need her. No satisfaction came from knowing she had done her job well. Instead an ache settled around her heart. She'd expected to have another month with Chad and Kara, but why should she? He would be foolish to keep her on now. The house looked as if she'd just cleaned it. He and Kara would only grow closer as he took over her care. She started out the door when Chad came down the hall.

"Mandy, are you just getting here?" He grinned at her. "We had a big day Saturday, didn't we?"

"The barn looks great." She glanced around the room. "So does the house. In fact, I don't see anything for me to do today. Maybe I should go home."

Chad chuckled. "You aren't trying to worm your way out of a job, are you? I thought you agreed to work for me through July."

"For what purpose?" Her voice sounded louder than she intended. "Face the truth, Chad. You don't need me. You and Kara are getting along fine, and you can obviously clean a house as well as I can. Maybe I should leave."

Before she knew he moved, Chad stood in front of her, holding her shoulders in his hands. He looked into her eyes; his voice was soft and low. "What are you talking about? How could I not need you? Did I do something that makes you think I lied to you about Susan?"

She shook her head at his questions and zeroed in on the last one. "No, you didn't do anything wrong. It's me. I can see you don't need me. You've taken care of the house and Kara, too, yesterday and this morning."

He gave a quick laugh. "Yesterday I took Kara to church and scarcely saw her until late afternoon when I left your folks' house. Between your sister and your mom, not to mention you and Brad's wife, I couldn't have gotten close to Kara if I'd tried."

When she started to speak, he stopped her. "No, I'm not complaining. I'm glad she's a cutie that everyone wants to play with. And I think it's great your mom treats her the same as she does her grandkids. Kara's soaking up the attention."

"You still had her last night and this morning. She's taking her nap, isn't she? Who put her to bed last night and this morning without help? Who cleaned up the kitchen after he fed her?" Amanda fought tears close to the surface. If she cried, Chad would know she didn't want to leave. She'd not felt so alone since she woke up and learned that Jeff and Charity had gone to heaven without her.

In spite of her resolve, one tear left her eye and rolled down her cheek. Chad pulled her to the sofa, and they sat together as he held her close. She sat in the comfort of his embrace for long seconds, fighting the tears that soon won. He patted her back until the storm of crying ended and she pulled away.

"I'm sorry, Chad. That was uncalled for. You can fire me if you want." She grabbed a tissue from a box on the coffee table and mopped up the evidence of her emotional display.

His chuckle brought a smile to her face. "I can't fire you yet, because I need to go buy some paint. Can you believe I bought all the lumber for the barn and forgot to get paint? I'd feel a lot better if someone either stayed with Kara or came along with me."

"And since she's sleeping now, I'd better stay here." Amanda smiled. Maybe he needed her a little bit still.

He kissed her lightly on the lips. "That's what I thought. I won't be gone long. Maybe an hour and a half. Will you be okay?"

Amanda sighed. "I'm fine. Just emotional."

"Then it wasn't anything to do with our past?" His eyes held vulnerability that touched Amanda's heart.

She shook her head.

"Have you forgiven me, Mandy? I know what I did was wrong, but—" He stopped and took a deep breath. "No, there are no excuses. Instead of wallowing in self-pity, I should've followed you to California and demanded you listen to me."

"You didn't know what Susan told me then." Amanda touched his hand, and his fingers curled around and through hers. "She was very good at deception, to you and to me. I should've known you would never force a woman, but I believed her story. Of course, I forgive you, but I need to be forgiven, too."

"Not in my opinion. She made sure you saw what she wanted you to see, and then she acted the part of the ravaged woman." He gave a short laugh. "I'd probably have believed her myself. But all you saw was an innocent hug that I thought was her consoling me because you wanted out of our engagement. She said you were going to dump me and go to California. Then you did."

"Because she convinced me I should." Amanda shook her head. "We were both so gullible."

After a short silence, Amanda looked into Chad's eyes. "I never thought I'd say this, but I'm glad I came back home. I believe God led me here, to help me let go of the past. I hold no ill feelings toward you or Susan. Not anymore. You were as innocent of wrongdoing as I was. She was a victim of her own sins. I hope she's figured that out by now."

"I always knew you were a better person than me." Chad's gaze held a touch of admiration.

Admiration she didn't deserve. She shook her head. "Only I'm not. I was angry for a long time. I didn't even know you and Susan supposedly married, because I refused to listen to anything about either of you. Even now I'm sorry it happened and that we didn't trust each other enough to stop her. But we can't look to the past. A verse in Philippians says, 'Forgetting what is behind and straining toward what is ahead, I press on toward the goal to win the prize for which God has called me heavenward in Christ Jesus.' That's what I want to do. I don't want to become burdened with the past. God has much better planned for our future than we ever had in the past."

His hand tightened around hers. "Are you saying there's a chance for us?"

She flinched from his question. She'd been thinking of heaven and he'd taken her words the wrong way. Did they have a future together? So much still kept them apart. What of Chad? He'd been reading the Bible, but did he serve the Lord? Had he ever been born again? At this point, she didn't know.

As if an arrow of wisdom pierced her mind, she saw the events of their past as stepping-stones laid out for Chad to come to a right relationship with the Lord. What of her? She, too, had stumbled through life saying she was a Christian, while she lived for herself. Only after sinking to the depths of grief for her husband and child had she started reaching upward to the One who gives true life. She continued daily to struggle with her journey toward God, so she couldn't judge Chad.

She met his questioning gaze without wavering. "I don't think we can answer that now, Chad. There's too much we don't know about each other."

"Then you aren't counting us out? If you need more time, that's fine." He looked around the room and back to her. "We're always working here or taking care of Kara, so we haven't spent much time together. Will you go out with me? On a date like we used to. Maybe we can get someone to watch Kara."

And tell him she couldn't have children? How would she find the words? How could she tell him she was no longer a complete woman? He'd back off and her heart would break for sure.

"I don't know, Chad." She stood, pulling her hand from his and missing the warmth. Still she crossed the room to stand inside the dining room. She held the back of a chair for support as she faced him. "Is that such a good idea?"

He stood but didn't move forward. "Your mom would watch her. Please ask her. We'll go this Friday afternoon to Springfield. Wouldn't you like to see the museum again? We'll go out to eat and take in a movie like we used to."

Oh, the temptation. Her fingers tightened around the chair back to keep from moving forward and exposing her heart by accepting. What he proposed meant they'd be together with no distractions for several hours. Alone with Chad. Time to explore their feelings and learn about each other. Yes, she wanted to.

She spoke from her heart. "I can ask."

He grinned. "Great. We'll plan on it then."

She couldn't stop her answering smile. He seemed so sure of himself, and he was probably right. Mom adored Kara. She'd welcome the chance to keep her for as long as she could. Mom liked Chad. Always had. Dad did, too. In fact her entire family acted like he'd come home when he spent Sundays with them.

He moved to the door and opened it. "I've got work to do. If you want something to keep you busy while Kara sleeps, you might go through the bookshelf in here. I took out a few books, but I don't want the rest. Take any you'd like and box up what's left. Do the same with the movies."

"Okay, I'll take a look. There's just a month left before I need to concentrate on school. I guess you'll be leaving for Rockford about then, too."

"Yeah, I guess so." He looked as glum as she felt. Then he shrugged. "We still have a month, and I've got to get some red paint. All barns are red, aren't they?"

She laughed. "Of course, that's why the color is called barn red."

"Good thinking." He went out the door with a smile.

Kara woke from her nap not long after Chad left. Amanda kept her busy inside until Chad's truck on the drive signaled his return two hours later. He came in for lunch then went to the barn and began the enormous task of painting the large building. She helped him paint that afternoon while Kara played and slept in her playpen in the fresh air.

Working with Chad and Kara brought the sense of family Amanda longed for. She loved Chad. He seemed to love her, too. He wanted to renew more than friendship by revisiting their old college haunts near old Route 66. She wanted to, too, but should she? Chad had always been a nice guy, but nice guys aren't always born-again Christians.

Pain ripped through her heart at the thought that Chad might be an unbeliever, but she had no assurance of anything different. The deeper her love for him grew, the harder it might become for her to walk close to the Lord.

That evening as she helped her mother clean the kitchen after they ate, she said, "Chad asked me to go with him to Springfield Friday afternoon."

"Oh really? What for?"

"The Lincoln Museum, dinner, a movie."

Mom turned from the sink and looked at her. "Doesn't that sound like a date to you?"

Amanda laughed. "Yeah, I kind of thought that's what he had in mind. He wanted me to ask you to watch Kara for us."

"I'd love to." Mom's smile faded. "But I won't be home from work until five and besides, are you sure this is a wise idea?"

Amanda's heart lurched at her mother's question. So she wasn't the only one concerned. She shrugged. "I don't know.

I love him, Mom. As much as I ever did. In fact, where it really counts, he hasn't changed much. He's still the kind, considerate man I knew fourteen years ago. I love talking to him, spending time with him."

"So what's the problem?" Mom turned and leaned against the sink, her arms crossed, her gaze searching Amanda's face.

Amanda pulled a kitchen chair out and sat down. "I don't know if he's a Christian, and I don't want to be unequally yoked. At least Jeff believed the same as I do."

The love she'd shared with Jeff couldn't compare to her feelings for Chad, but Jeff had been a dedicated Christian man. He'd been good to her, and he'd loved her in his own way. She'd had a good marriage. If and when she married again, she wanted an even better one. One like she and Chad could have if they both served the Lord.

"Maybe you shouldn't go." Mom's eyebrows raised in that you'd-better-listen-to-me expression Amanda recognized. "If there's doubt in your mind, there's a reason. You are right to be cautious. We can't always go by our feelings. Pray about this, Amanda. If you have peace, I'll watch Kara. If not, you'll have to tell him no."

Mom was right, but that didn't stop disappointment from weighing heavily on Amanda. She'd pray just as she'd been doing, and tomorrow she'd tell Chad she couldn't go. God had been dealing with her about getting too close to Chad. He wouldn't likely change His mind just because she asked Him again.

fifteen

A blanket of clouds overhead and rain on her windshield matched Amanda's mood as she stopped behind Chad's truck. They wouldn't be painting the barn today. In fact, she probably didn't need to be here. They'd be celebrating the Fourth of July in less than a week. If she stayed home, she could find plenty to do preparing for her family's annual barbecue.

With a sigh pulled from the depths of her soul, she opened the car door and ran to the porch. After a quick knock on the door, she opened it and stepped inside.

"You running from a little water?" Chad appeared in the dining room doorway with a wide grin.

Kara had been crawling across the living room floor, but now stopped and sat watching her. She squealed and clapped her hands. "Mama."

Amanda's mouth fell open as she looked at Chad.

He laughed. "Sounds like you got promoted. Hey, stay there by the door. I want you to see this."

With a couple of long strides, he crossed the floor and picked Kara up. He carried her to the opposite side of the living room from Amanda and knelt. Standing Kara in front of him, he said, "Now hold out your hands and see if she'll come to you."

Amanda's heart pounded. Kara could walk? She'd been close several times, but Amanda hadn't let her go for selfish reasons. Walking turned a baby into a toddler, and she didn't know if she was ready to lose her baby. As if Kara would ever be hers. Chad obviously had no such qualms.

She did as Chad asked and crouched down about six feet from them with her hands reaching. "Come here, Kara. Come to Manda."

Kara squealed again and stiffened in Chad's hands before taking a tentative step forward. He loosened his hold and, keeping his hands a few inches to either side of her, followed her as she took several more steps before wobbling.

He started to catch her, but she plopped to the floor with a wide grin and crawled rapidly the rest of the way into Amanda's hands. Amanda caught her up into her arms and held her close for a kiss. She blinked her eyes. "You're such a big girl. If I cry it's only because I can't stand the thought of you getting all grown up."

She looked up to see Chad watching them with an almost smile on his face. Their eyes caught and held. He lifted one shoulder in a shrug. "You could watch her grow up, you know."

Tears rushed to her eyes and she brushed them away, breaking contact with him. "No, Chad. Don't say that. You have a life in Rockford. My job is here. In four short weeks you'll be gone."

"What about Friday night?" He hesitated. "Did you ask your mom?"

She nodded.

"And?"

She sighed and, after another hug, set Kara down beside her toys. "I talked to her and told her my concerns. She suggested I pray about everything, which I did."

When she didn't continue, Chad said, "So you think God cares who you date? Marriage, maybe—and yeah, I admit I want to marry you, Mandy—but Friday is just a date. That's all I'm asking right now. Just some time to talk and be together without distractions."

Tears threatened. Amanda hated crying just as she hated

the conflict his confession placed on her. Her heart leaped at the thought of being Chad's wife and Kara's mother then sank with a burden of regret because she couldn't. She pulled a tissue from the box on the coffee table and dabbed her eyes.

"You want to go, don't you?" He knew her too well.

She nodded but wouldn't look at him.

"Then why won't you?"

Her head jerked up as her eyes met his frowning but beloved face. She kept her voice soft for Kara's sake. "Don't you understand how torn inside I am? I can't go with my feelings, Chad. I have to do what's right. I have to let you both go."

"I don't see that, Mandy. We're two halves of a whole that need to be back together. You can't tell me your life is complete without me. I won't believe you. I know mine isn't and never has been. Without you, I'm only existing."

"Without Christ, you are only existing. I can't make you complete, Chad. Only Jesus Christ can do that. Do you know Him as your personal savior?"

There. She'd laid everything out before him. She hadn't intended to, but maybe the timing was more right than she knew. She waited while a muscle twitched in his jaw.

He shook his head. "Now you sound like Jessica. When we were kids, I went to church as much as she did. So I got away from all that for a while. I've always tried to live right and treat everyone the way I wanted to be treated. I messed up with Susan. I admit that, but does that make me so bad? I asked your forgiveness. What more do you want, Amanda? A full confession of everything I've ever done?"

She shook her head while his words added weight to her heart. "No I don't, Chad. God does. 'If we confess our sins, He is faithful and just and will forgive us our sins and purify us from all unrighteousness.' First John 1:9."

He gave a short laugh and spoke under his breath. "So now I'm unrighteous."

Amanda didn't know what to say. She breathed a quick prayer for guidance, but Chad spoke first.

He stood and glanced out the window. "You know I don't think the rain's going to let up anytime soon. Maybe we need some time apart. I've got things covered here, so if you want to go home, that's fine."

He was angry with her. The muscle in his jaw stayed clenched. But he was right, too. They did need time apart. She'd messed everything up by her impulsive attempt to witness to him. As soon as she got home, if she didn't start crying and feeling sorry for herself, she'd spend some serious time in prayer.

She stood, too. "I think you're right. I'm sorry if I said anything to offend you, but what I said was the truth. I do love you, but God loves you so much more."

"Yeah, sure Amanda. I know. I'm not a stranger to church or the Bible." His cell phone rang and he jerked it from his pocket. "Hello?" He walked through the dining room into the kitchen, leaving Kara on the floor.

Amanda decided she'd better stay and keep an eye on Kara until he returned, so she sank to the sofa to wait.

Within a few minutes he was back, and his eyes widened when he looked at her. "I'm glad you waited. That was a real estate agent in Rockford. She's found a couple of houses she thinks I might like, so I've decided to go back early."

Amanda straightened. "What do you mean? Are you buying a house up there?"

He shrugged. "Yeah, I thought about it. There won't be enough room in my one-bedroom apartment for Kara. A house may be more than we need now, but I probably should get up there and get things settled before school."

Amanda stood. "I see. When are you leaving?"

"By noon tomorrow."

His answer hit her like a blow to the stomach. Why so

soon? To get away from her, of course.

"Please, may I come back tomorrow to tell Kara good-bye?"

He looked from her to the baby who crawled over and pulled up on his leg. He picked her up, and Amanda knew she was no longer needed. He'd the same as said so. Still she needed that last few minutes with them both before they left. Even if they couldn't be in her life, she would love them both forever.

He nodded. "Sure. We didn't get everything packed up, but I don't imagine it's necessary yet. Not many people want to buy a house that's in the path of tornadoes, so I doubt it'll sell too soon."

"You may be right." Amanda gave Kara a quick kiss and hug before she turned back to the door and this time went outside. Chad didn't follow her, but she heard Kara's voice calling, "Mama."

ஐ

Chad stood where she'd left him, aching for her. He held Kara close and patted her back as she continued calling for "Mama."

What'd she been talking about, anyway? Saying he needed to tell God everything he'd ever done. In the first place, God already knew everything. In the second place, the only really bad thing he'd ever done was believe Susan and give in to her seduction when he missed Amanda so much he couldn't think straight. God knew he was sorry for that.

He made a disgusted sound and turned to the kitchen. "How would you like to have a cracker?"

He put Kara in her high chair and gave her a graham cracker. Thankful when she took it and her tears for Amanda stopped, he turned to the kitchen cabinets. After several minutes of opening and closing doors and drawers, he turned away. Everything looked fine where it was. He took Kara out of the high chair, gave her another cracker, and went to the back of the house where Amanda had some things boxed up. Might as well see what was in them before he took them to storage. He needed to find a real estate agent and list the farm, anyway.

While Kara played on the floor and smeared her cracker all over her face and clothes, he opened boxes. Two held quilts he figured his sister had made. He'd keep those. The third box was heavy. There were some novels on top and a few cookbooks. He set them aside and pulled out a picture album. With dread and curiosity mingling, he opened the cover and leaned back against the wall as memories rose from the pages. He recognized Jessica's handwriting where she'd labeled each picture.

She must have gotten Mom's albums because the first page held their baby pictures. His and Jessica's. Until that moment he hadn't realized how much Kara looked like her mother. There were pictures of his dad and mom. One must have been taken on Easter Sunday because all four of them were dressed especially nice as they stood outside the little country church they'd attended before they moved to town after Dad died.

He turned the pages and felt more alone than he ever had in his life. His eyes burned, and he fought the emotions he'd put down for so long. He wanted to push the album away, but the pictures called to him until he couldn't. By the time he reached Jessica and Steve's wedding pictures, his heart seemed to have grown double its normal size and was just as heavy. Mom looked happy.

He closed his eyes and leaned his head against the wall. She'd died two months later. Cancer crept in and took her life. Silent tears slid down his face. He turned another page and there was Jessica in the hospital with newborn Kara in her arms and Steve holding them both close. Their faces shone with wonder and love for the gift they held, for Kara truly was a precious gift from God. Theirs for ten months. Already they'd been gone almost two months.

A tear dropped to the page beside the picture, so he closed the book, letting it slide from his lap. Another tear fell and then another. He bowed his head as his heart burst with sorrow and loss. Deep sobs of grief such as he had never cried before tore from him. He cried for his dad and his mom. He cried for Jessica and Steve, and he cried for Amanda. For the love they once had, but lost. For the second chance he'd somehow blown without knowing how or why.

He cried until he felt a weight on his leg, and his sweet child climbed on his lap. She patted his face and said, "Dada?" Her innocence and acceptance of him brought a fresh wave of tears, only silent now. Then she cried, too. Not so silently. He hugged her close and patted her back while his tears stopped falling. He wiped his face with his shirtsleeve and took a deep breath. He hadn't cried like that in years. In fact, maybe never. He hoped never again.

He got up and took Kara to the kitchen where he fixed her a bottle of milk using only one hand. She latched on to her bottle and lay back in his arms with her eyes drooping. He grinned. "Looks like we've got a date with a rocking chair, little girl."

❧

The early morning sun reflected from a real estate sign on the edge of Chad's property as Amanda drove past. She gripped the steering wheel. *Lord, why? Why did You bring us back together and then tear us apart? If Chad was a Christian, he'd have said so yesterday. Instead he got angry. 'In all things God works for the good of those who love Him.' Let this be one of those things. Please Lord, even if Chad and I can't be together, at least bring him to You.*

Amanda knocked on the door and heard Chad call out, "Come on in."

She found Kara playing with some toys in the middle of the floor. The little girl squealed when she saw her and crawled to meet her. Amanda scooped her up and gave her a hug. "I missed you, sweetie. One day away from you and I can't wait to be back. What will I do after today?"

She looked up to find Chad's gaze on her. He didn't speak but turned away, picked up a couple of boxes, and walked out the door with them. While she played with Kara, he made several trips from the bedrooms to his truck. Not once did he speak, and she didn't try to get him to. Finally he stood in the doorway watching her and Kara play with a toy telephone. She sat back on her heels on the floor and looked up at him.

"Soon as I lock up the house, I'm ready to go." No emotion moved across his face.

"All right." She stood and picked Kara and her telephone up. "I'll buckle Kara in for you. Do you have a bottle for her? Diapers and wipes handy? It's a long drive."

Her voice caught on the last sentence, but he didn't seem to notice. He nodded. "It's all taken care of. Thanks for all your help. Oh, here's your pay through today."

She stared at the envelope he held out. What would he do if she refused to take it? At first she didn't mind taking his money. Actually she hadn't thought much about it one way or another, but the last few weeks had been hard taking pay for doing something she loved. Maybe it was a good thing the job was over, because it had never been a real job to her anyway. She'd been playing house. Only the house didn't belong to her. Neither did the man or the child.

She took the envelope and stuffed it in the hip pocket of her jeans. "Thanks. I'll take Kara out."

By sheer force of will, Amanda held her tears until Chad locked the house and joined her and Kara at the truck. She backed away and watched him slide behind the wheel. With the door still open, his eyes met hers and she recognized her own pain reflected in them.

When he spoke, his words were like knives slicing through her heart. "I won't be buying a house. I'll probably just look for a larger apartment. The house was for us before I knew. . ." His voice broke and he cleared his throat. "Well anyway, Kara and I can get by with a bigger apartment. Thanks, Amanda, for your help. I couldn't have handled this without you. I guess this is good-bye."

She couldn't speak for the knot in her throat, so she nodded and stepped back. He pulled his door closed, and she fled to her car.

Why did doing the right thing hurt so much?

sixteen

She was home before noon. Mom and Dad always took lunches or ate out, and she didn't feel like fixing anything for herself. The house felt cool compared to the summer sun outdoors. Cool, dark, and empty. She stood in her parents' spacious living room and held her arms tight across her middle. She'd already cried a bucket of tears. She'd prayed until she had no more words to give. And still her heart cried out to the Father. *Please bring him to You, Lord. Not for me, but for You and for him. May Chad find the joy of salvation.*

She took a deep, calming breath. Less than a week until the Fourth of July. Mom could use her help. She could use the distraction. She headed toward the kitchen where Mom kept her to-do list. There'd be plenty to keep her busy this week.

"I'd like to help serve at the barbecue this year," Amanda told her folks that night and watched her dad's eyebrows rise. She smiled. "So I don't usually volunteer, but Sarah and Kevin can't come because her morning sickness is just now starting to go away, and she's afraid the drive would stir things up again. Tessa says Blake's opening another restaurant in Lubbock, Texas, and they don't have time to come. What else can I do? I might as well help where I can."

"We'll put you to work, honey." Mom patted her back as she set the bowl of potatoes on the table. "Now let's eat, and I'll tell you all sorts of things you can do. In fact, I'll have you so busy, you won't be able to think."

She laughed with her parents but saw the underlying sympathy in their eyes and looked away. She'd make it through this. School would keep her busy soon. In fact she'd be attending an orientation seminar in a couple of weeks.

The next few days passed quickly, while the nights stretched forever. The Davis family's Fourth of July barbecue drew a large crowd as usual. Brad, Esther, and their kids were there. So were Karen and Wayne and their two girls. Amanda felt alone in the crowd until her brother and sister cornered her.

"Hey, you doing okay?" Brad lightly clipped her shoulder with his fist.

She shrugged. "Sure, Mom's keeping me busy. Didn't you see me serving desserts?"

"Yeah, I thought about taking a picture to make sure I wasn't seeing things." Brad grinned. "What happened to hiding when the jobs get handed out?"

Karen laughed. "Oh Brad, be nice. Amanda's grown up now. She doesn't run from work anymore. So rather than beat around the bush, why don't we just ask what we want to know?"

Amanda looked from her sister to her brother. They both watched her. "What is this? Gang up on little Amanda? Didn't you two outgrow that about twenty years ago?"

"Nope." Brad grinned. "As your big brother—"

"And your big sister—" Karen added.

"It's our duty to make sure you aren't being hurt," Brad finished. "So, what happened between you and Chad? I heard he left town all of a sudden."

They meant well. They were also annoying older siblings. Amanda laughed and muttered, "I can't believe this."

"He's a good guy, Amanda." Karen crossed her arms as if she expected a denial.

Amanda nodded. "He's a good guy who needs to accept salvation."

"He isn't a born-again Christian?" Karen's mouth opened

and she stared at Brad. "I thought. . .Mom said he went to church, and he's so nice."

Brad shrugged.

Amanda looked from one to the other of her caring siblings. "I may as well pour out my heart to you two. Here's the bottom line. I love Chad more than I've ever loved any other man, including Jeff, although I did love him. I love Kara as if she were my own child. My second child."

She crossed her arms and blinked. "If I had peace in my heart about this, I would marry him like yesterday and move to Rockford. But I don't. It would be a mistake, so I let him go. Now I'm getting on with my life. I have a job, and I plan to be the best kindergarten teacher this school has ever had. End of story."

&

After the confrontation with her brother and sister on the Fourth, Amanda poured her energy into getting on with her life. But eight days after the barbecue was especially hard for Amanda. Kara turned one year old that day. She drove to the empty farmhouse and sat in the driveway. Because she'd opened her mouth and offended Chad, she'd missed celebrating with the little girl who seemed so much a part of her. Charity had never reached her first birthday, and now Kara was gone, too.

Sobs shook her body as she longed to hold her daughter, and somehow the two girls blended into one until she didn't know which she grieved for the most— Charity or Kara.

When she returned from the orientation seminar a few weeks later, she began visits with her future students in their homes. She worked in her classroom and prepared lesson plans and materials. Her life was more than full, yet not a day went by that she didn't miss Chad and Kara.

Then, on the first day of school, she met a fellow teacher who reminded her of Jeffrey. When he caught her eye and smiled with a quick wink, her heart stuttered from a memory long ago when Jeff had done the same thing the first time they met. Maybe she hadn't shriveled up and died inside like she'd thought.

❧

Chad returned to the apartment after the first day of school and pulled his tie off as soon as the door closed behind him.

"Is that you, Mr. Randall?" Velma called from the kitchen.

Who else would it be? He didn't let his foul mood sound in his voice. "Yeah, it's me."

He rounded the corner to the combination kitchen/dining room and saw a homey scene that only served to emphasize Amanda's absence from their lives. His housekeeper, who was at least fifty, stood at the table stirring something in a bowl. Cookies probably, since Kara had a homemade sugar cookie clutched in one hand and cookie crumbs strewn from her face to the floor. She welcomed him with a messy smile and banged her cookie on the tray, scattering more crumbs.

He laughed at the sight. "So are we having cookies for dinner?"

Velma laughed. "There's fish in the oven, mashed potatoes and broccoli on the counter, salad in the refrigerator, and cookies for dessert along with some ice cream if you'd like."

"Sounds good to me." He didn't much care what he ate. Or if he did. As long as Kara was taken care of. And Velma did a good job of that as far as he could see. Only she was more grandma than mother substitute. Kara needed Amanda. He needed Amanda. His heart ached for her every minute of every day.

❧

He wasn't surprised Sunday morning when his first thought was to get ready for church. But why should he? He'd gone last Sunday and the preacher had sounded like Amanda, saying a man had to be born again or he couldn't go to heaven.

Why go listen to all the things he'd heard since he was a kid? Sometimes he felt as if a battle raged inside him. He'd started reading his Bible more than he ever had. Jessica's Bible, actually. He liked reading the notes she'd written in the margins because they made him feel closer to her. And they stirred something inside him to be more like her.

He threw the covers back and got out of bed. What would it hurt to go to church? Jessica and Steve would want Kara raised in church. He might not know much about being a parent, but his parents seldom missed church. He took a shower and dressed.

When he lifted Kara from bed, she felt warm and didn't greet him with her usual smile. His heart lurched. She couldn't be sick. What would he do with her sick on Sunday? He changed her diaper and dressed her, then carried her into the living room and sat in his recliner while he dialed Velma's number.

"Hello?"

His breath rushed out. "Velma, this is Chad Randall. Kara's warm and fussy. Do you have any ideas what might be wrong?"

Her chuckle did little to reassure him. "I'd guess it's her teeth. I thought she acted like her gum was hurting on Friday. I'm getting ready for church, but Fred will bring me by your apartment if you want me to take a look."

Chad leaned his head back against the chair and felt the tension ease. "No, you don't need to go out of your way. A drive might soothe her, so why don't I bring her by your house? I can be there in a few minutes."

"Come by if you want, but you can check for yourself. Wash your hands really good and touch her lower gum beside her teeth. She'll either clamp down or jerk back." Velma sounded confident, so Chad did as she said.

Sure enough, Kara bit down on his finger and chewed.

Amazingly, her fussing stopped. He called Velma back. "You were right. So how do I help her? She can't keep chewing on my finger."

Velma laughed. "Get her a teething ring and a bottle of teething lotion. A children's pain reliever will help, too. Won't be long until we have a new tooth."

"Thanks, Velma." Chad clicked off his phone and leaned back in his chair for a moment. *Amanda, why aren't you here with me? You'd know what to do for her.*

With a quick shake of his head, he stood with Kara still gumming his finger. Poor baby. The sooner he got something to ease the pain, the better. He carried her out to his truck and drove to the store. After he paid for his purchases, he went into the men's room and thoroughly washed the teething ring before giving it to Kara. Then he gave her a dose of nonaspirin liquid pain medicine, put the remainder back in the bag, and left the store.

On the way home he drove past the street that led to the church he'd attended the week before. On impulse, he turned at the next corner and went around the block. "Do you want to go to church, Kara?"

A quick check in the rearview mirror showed a contented baby still chewing on her new plastic ring. Amazing. Maybe they could sit in the back, and if she started fussing again, they could leave. Sounded reasonable to him.

Reasonable, but not comfortable. Again, the minister talked about the necessity of salvation, the need to make a commitment to Christ. Chad looked down at the sleeping baby in his arms and tried to find a more comfortable position. He rested his elbow on the armrest. Jessica had often urged him to walk the walk, as she called it. To return to the beliefs of their youth.

Like Amanda, she thought he was a heathen because he didn't attend church all the time. He'd been going more over the summer and since he returned home than he had in the last fourteen years. Did that count? Maybe not. Something nagged at him deep inside as if a weight were pulling down on his heart.

The minister's voice penetrated his thoughts. "In Hebrews 9:27 and 28, we read, 'Just as people are destined to die once, and after that to face judgment, so Christ was sacrificed once to take away the sins of many.' Will you die someday? God's Word says that day is appointed for you and for me."

Words from the pulpit beat into Chad's mind with frightening clarity. People died daily. Young or old, it made no difference. Jessica stepped out the door of her house and never returned. In a matter of minutes the tornado destroyed her barn and took her and Steve into eternity. With an assurance that didn't waver, Chad knew his sister and brother-in-law were in heaven. If he had been taken in their place, where would he be? As a preteen, he'd asked Jesus into his heart, but had he ever committed his life in service to Christ? No, he'd gone his own way, living the way he wanted without a thought for God's way. Had he ever really been saved?

"Do you feel Jesus knocking at your heart's door?" The minister stepped down and held out his hand. "Come, let us pray with you."

Chad's heart pounded as he held Kara close. She still slept. He couldn't wake her. Not after she'd been in so much pain. Thankfully, she didn't feel warm now. He didn't need to go forward for prayer, anyway. He shifted in his seat then stood with the congregation. Church would soon be over.

Kara woke as Chad shook hands with the minister at the back door after dismissal. The older man said, "I'm so glad to see you again. Please, make yourself at home here."

Chad nodded and smiled. "Thank you. I plan to come when I can."

"We'll count on it. And this young lady, too." He smiled and touched Kara's tiny hand. "You're a sweetheart, aren't you?"

By the time Chad worked his way through several women who wanted to speak to Kara, he was ready to head home. As they walked across the parking lot, Kara said, "Mama."

"Who are you talking about, baby?" He frowned. *You don't have a mama. Your first mama died, and Mandy walked away from us.* The bright September sun did nothing to brighten his life.

Throughout the second week of school, Chad forced himself to concentrate on the history lessons as he lectured and gave out assignments. Wednesday, he warned his class, "There will be a test Friday over the material we've studied so far. It's not an important part of your grade, but it will give you points you may be thankful for later. Also save these short tests to use as a study guide for the longer tests. Doing your best now will pay off in the long run."

Even as the words left his mouth, he felt a tug in his soul. What was his best? The answer came as if spoken to him. *"Love the Lord your God with all your heart and with all your soul and with all your mind and with all your strength."* Had he memorized this verse as a child? Probably. He'd look it up tonight. See if Jessica had written any comments in the margin.

He did look up the verse and found it in Mark 12:30. In Jessica's handwriting, he read, *How can I do less than love Him with everything that is in me? He gave everything for me. Without Him I would not exist. Jesus, I love You.*

He didn't know he was crying until a tear fell on his hand. Longing he'd fought since he drove away from the farm pressed against him. Amanda. His love for her would never leave. Seeing her again had brought her back to him in a way he could no longer ignore. Surely she was the cause of this emptiness inside his heart.

Thursday he made arrangements for a substitute teacher to take his classes the next day. Soon he would see Mandy, and then everything would be set right.

He rose early Friday morning. Kara must've sensed his excitement, because she woke early, too. Why wait any longer? They headed south as soon as he packed a couple of bags and fed Kara.

As he drove, Kara went to sleep, and the silence in the truck became a perfect breeding ground for troubling thoughts to grow in his mind. The comments from Jessica's Bible and the verses he'd learned as a child brought back the restless feelings he'd fought for two weeks. He snapped on the radio, hoping for a distraction. An old song, beautifully sung, filled the cab of his truck: "Amazing Grace, how sweet the sound that saved a wretch like me. I once was lost, but now I'm found—"

He twisted the dial, cutting off the music, as sweat broke out on his forehead. What was going on? He couldn't get away from this. A rest area appeared ahead, and he took the exit, parking away from other vehicles. He leaned his head against the steering wheel and cried. "Lord Jesus, help me. I need You."

seventeen

Amanda watched her last small student board the bus that would take him home, then turned and walked back to her classroom. She picked up a wadded paper from the floor and tossed it into the wastebasket. The last few weeks had proved one thing to her, or maybe two things. She loved teaching almost as much as she missed Chad and Kara. She stepped behind her desk and faced the door. If he walked through that door, she'd throw herself into his arms and never let go.

At that moment a man stepped through the open doorway, and she gasped, her heart racing.

"Hello, Amanda." Dan Hunt smiled at her and pushed his glasses into place as he neared her desk.

Her breath left in a rush, and she plopped into the chair behind her. "Hi."

"How's kindergarten?" He leaned against the wall and folded his arms as if he planned to stay awhile.

"Fine. Fun, actually." She straightened and pushed Chad from her mind. She couldn't let a fantasy rule her life. "And what about your domain? How's sixth-grade science?"

He grinned. "This year has all the earmarks of the three W's. Wild, weird, but wonderful. Can't think of a thing I'd rather be doing. Well, except for one."

"Really? What would that be?" Not that she cared.

His eyes appeared large behind his glasses. He blinked. "Dinner with a beautiful woman. How about it, Amanda? Will you go with me?"

Had he just asked her out? On a date? Dan was nice. In fact, he was a wonderful Christian man, and he did remind her of Jeff in an abstract sort of way. Maybe she should go out with him and forget Chad. Why not?

She opened her mouth to accept but lost the ability to speak when Chad stepped into her classroom. Unless her longing and dreams had brought him to life, Chad Randall stood two steps inside her room smiling at her. Kara sat on his arm looking from one bright display to another.

Amanda stood and walked around her desk. *Don't let them disappear. Please Lord, let this be real.*

She saw movement from the corner of her eye. Dan! She'd forgotten all about him. She turned to apologize and explain.

Then Kara saw her. And squealed. "Mama."

The baby lunged and Chad grabbed her to keep her from falling. Amanda ran to them and lifted her into her arms where she belonged. She squeezed her close, laughing and crying at the same time. She couldn't stop but covered Kara's face with her kisses.

"Hey, save some of that for me." Chad growled, but his eyes looked especially bright, and his smile grew wider.

"Oh Chad." Amanda stepped home as his arms drew her close. His lips barely touched hers as if he were asking permission. Her response must have been the answer he needed as the kiss deepened.

She pulled back to look into the face of her dreams and search for answers. "Why are you here?"

"We came for the weekend."

"Oh, to check on the farm?" She started to pull back, but he wouldn't let her.

"Sure, we'll go to the farm, but this was our first stop." He still held her in the circle of his arms. "You're our first priority, Mandy. Always will be. Don't you know yet how much I love you and always have?"

She looked at a button on his chest. "I think so, but. . ."

He chuckled. "There've been some changes. Are you

finished here? Kara's hungry and I'm starved. Let's go eat somewhere so I can tell you everything."

They left Amanda's car and stopped at Sonic. After he prayed over their food, Chad told Amanda about his experience at the roadside park. "I met the Lord for the first time today, Mandy. I was raised in church, but I never accepted the sacrifice He made for me until today."

Amanda gave him a soft smile. "I'm glad, Chad. Too many people think lip service is all that's required. Christ gave everything for us, why can't we understand He deserves and even demands our all in return?"

"I understand what you're saying." Chad smiled. "I thought I was all right until you challenged me. I've been going to church in Rockford, but I still resisted God's call. In fact, I started down here today to talk you into marrying me. I thought that was the cause of my unrest. I thought I needed you to make me complete. I still need you. That'll never change. But. . .I don't know."

He shook his head. "After I prayed back at that park, it's like I made a complete turnaround. I'm not like I was, Mandy. Do you know what I'm talking about?"

"'Therefore if anyone is in Christ, he is a new creation; the old has gone, the new has come!'" She smiled. "Yes, I understand exactly what you're talking about. I feel as if these last few minutes have been a dream come true."

Chad chuckled. "Then how about making my dream come true?"

Amanda's breath caught while her sandwich lay on her lap untouched. Her heart danced in place. "Your dream?"

He nodded. "And yours, I hope. More than fourteen years ago, we were supposed to get married. Don't you think we've waited long enough?"

The intensity in his eyes held her in place as she nodded.

"I hope that means yes."

"Yes?" How could she answer without the question he hadn't asked?

He said he was starved, but he hadn't so much as touched his food. He took her hands in his, as she faced him. "Mandy, you hold my heart in your hands. I've never felt so vulnerable, so scared. How many times does a man have to ask the woman he loves if she'll marry him before it really happens? Mandy, will you marry me?"

"Yes. As soon as possible." He started to pull her forward for a kiss, but she cried out, "No, I can't."

Distress drew her brows together. How could she have forgotten? She bowed her head and tried to pull her hands back, but he wouldn't let go. "I can't marry anyone."

"Why?"

She owed him an explanation. What did she have to lose now? She'd already lost him. She relaxed her hands. He'd let go soon enough. With a show of courage she didn't feel, she met his gaze and opened her heart to rejection.

"I lost more in the accident than a husband and child, Chad." He watched her in silence. She spoke barely above a whisper. "I was hurt inside. By the time I woke up enough to know what had happened, I'd had a few operations, including a hysterectomy. I can't have children."

His expression softened, and he released her hands to slip his arms around her shoulders. He pulled her as close as he could in the confines of the truck cab. Without a word, he kissed her face, her cheeks, and her forehead. Then he kissed her lips and with another hug pulled back to look into her eyes. "Do you honestly think I'm marrying you for children?"

"Are you saying that isn't important?"

He shook his head. "We aren't kids anymore, Mandy. Besides, if you'll look in the backseat, you'll find a child. Why don't we just take that one and raise her as ours? In fact, why don't we adopt her so she's ours legally? She already calls us Mama and Dada."

Tears sprang to Amanda's eyes. Tears of joy rather than rejection. She laughed and nodded.

Chad chuckled. "I hope that means what I think it does."

"It means yes, I'll marry you. As soon as possible." She threw her hand over her mouth. "But what about school? I have a contract."

"That could be a problem, but we'll figure something out. First thing Monday see what it takes to get out of your contract. That leaves us this weekend to pray for God's will. I guarantee He's got it covered."

"Oh Chad, I love you." Amanda took the initiative and kissed him. When she pulled away, she remembered something. "When you came into my classroom, was there a man there?"

Chad chuckled. "Don't you remember?"

She shook her head. "He was there before, but I didn't see him leave. I started to apologize to him, but Kara called me mama. Did he leave?"

"He left." Chad grinned. "He acted surprised by our presence. I guess he didn't know you already had a family."

"Oh dear." Amanda looked in the backseat where Kara sat quietly shredding the bun from her sandwich. "I can imagine the rumors that will be going around next week."

"Who was he? An erstwhile suitor?"

Amanda giggled. "He'd just asked me out to dinner. I think he had something a little different than this in mind, too."

Chad dug in his pants pocket. "I brought some wolf repellent with me. I want you to wear it all the time. If it doesn't keep guys like him away, let me know, and I'll make sure they don't bother you."

Wolf repellent? Mace? Amanda's heart set up its tap dance again when she recognized the jeweler's box in his hand.

"You gave your ring to Susan, and I guess she deserves some credit for returning it to me. Although that was probably part of her plan, too." He opened the box and Amanda forgot to breathe.

The wedding set he'd bought while they were in college sparkled as if the rings had only now come from the store. He lifted the engagement ring out and snapped the box closed, hiding the two matching wedding rings, one for her, one for him. He held her left hand and positioned the beautiful solitaire over her third finger. "Just so you know, Susan never saw this ring after she returned it. I kept them, not because I thought this day would ever come, but because they were all I had left of you besides memories and pictures. God has restored what the tempter took. Do you have any objections to using our original rings?"

Amanda's breath rushed in with her nod. "Yes, no."

She laughed. "Thank you. I want my ring back. I love you."

"I love you, Mandy. Always and forever." With that declaration, he returned her ring to its rightful place.

❧

Sunday morning, Chad gave his testimony of God's saving grace before the church. He stood to the side of the pulpit, looking so handsome Amanda wanted to stand and tell everyone he was hers.

"I especially want to thank this church for everything you've done for me and Kara." Chad looked out over the congregation. "I've learned a valuable lesson from your example. Maybe you didn't know what you were doing last May when you drove to Lakeland and volunteered to help clean up after the tornadoes that ripped through the area. But God knew. He directed you to me and to Kara. We needed you for more than removing a tree from the house and fixing the roof. For cleaning up the yard and the house. A brand-new barn stands now as a testimony of this church's missionary vision. You reached out and performed miracles, but you let God work through you to bring about the greatest miracle of all. That of a sinner saved by God's grace. From the bottom of my heart, thank you for that."

≈

Saturday morning Chad and Amanda stood in the Lakeland Cemetery before the two graves. Already new grass covered the disturbed ground. Chad knelt with Kara in his arms to see the headstones. He traced the lettering as he talked to his fourteen-month-old niece.

"Kara, we can't see your mommy and daddy now because they live with Jesus, but we can come here and feel close to them because this is where their bodies are. Someday we'll join them in heaven. I know you've already forgotten so much about them, but I promise I'll do my best to help you remember and know how much they loved you."

Kara babbled words known only to her. Chad hugged her and looked up at Amanda. She laid her hand on his shoulder, love for him and Kara filling her heart. A verse in the Old Testament came to her mind. "I will repay you for the years the locusts have eaten. . ." Surely God had given back what had been taken from them.

epilogue

Late Saturday after Thanksgiving, Amanda stood at the closed double doors leading into the sanctuary of her home church. Her dress was not the extravagant, typical wedding attire, but she wore a simple pale green gown that touched the floor and brought out the green of her eyes and the red highlights in her hair. Or so Sarah said. She'd been thrilled when both her best friends, Tessa and Sarah, had made the trip to her wedding just as they'd promised they would.

Tessa steered Sarah toward the door. "You'd better give that baby to your mom before you have to carry her down the aisle."

"Oh no you don't," Amanda said. "Not until I get one more kiss."

"Why do I think you would spoil my daughter if you lived close enough?" Sarah held little Andrea Nichols close to Amanda.

Amanda touched her tiny hand and kissed her forehead as she slept. She smiled at Sarah. "Because I would. I'll be out of reach in Rockford, though, so you can rest easy. Looks like I'll be staying home this winter with my own little one."

Kara stood to the side with her new cousins, who were older, but still young enough to be quite fascinating to a sixteen-month-old.

"How'd you get out of your teaching contract, anyway?" Tessa asked.

Amanda shrugged. "It pays to know people. Linda has a friend. A retired teacher who missed the classroom and needed the money. She was glad to take over the rest of the year. She sat in on the class with me this last week and seems very nice. The kids took to her right off. Chad and I will both be applying back this way for next year."

"Then you'll live here?" Sarah asked.

Amanda smiled at her two best friends. "We have a farm that sits close to Route 66. We thought we'd like to stay in the area."

Sarah gave her a quick hug. "We'll get together more often then. I'm so glad."

Linda slipped through the door and took her grand-daughter from Sarah. With a smile and wink for Amanda, she went back into the sanctuary.

"Amazing, isn't it?" Tessa said. "The three of us. I mean, what is it with the Mother Road and second chances? You'd think there might be something special about the road itself."

Amanda nodded. "Maybe there is. But I think Someone had a hand in each of us coming back where we belong. He just used Route 66 to bring it about."

"That's true." Karen turned from talking to her dad to add her opinion. "Considering Chad, Sarah, Kevin, and Blake all became Christians because of it."

"Amen," Sarah murmured.

"I agree." Tessa nodded. "Thank God for what He has done."

The church organ had been playing softly. Now the tune changed, and they took their places. Tessa stood in front of the door waiting, while Karen moved closer to Amanda and their dad.

Amanda said, "Tessa, we're right behind you."

Tessa grinned over her shoulder. "You aren't nervous, are you?"

Amanda waved her forward with both hands and gave an exaggerated nod as Tessa laughed. But then the ushers opened the doors and Tessa began the long walk to the front with Sarah not far behind. Karen followed ahead of Brad's daughter and son who carried a basket of flowers and a pillow cushioning the rings. Karen's girls came next, each holding one of Kara's hands as she toddled between them. As she went through the door, she looked back at Amanda and said, "Bye, bye, Mama."

"Bye, precious. I'm coming right behind you." Amanda smiled at her dad when he patted her hand on his arm.

"I'm proud of you, Amanda." He spoke in a soft voice. "You're getting another good man."

"I know, Dad. God has blessed me twice in spite of my failings."

He simply nodded as they stepped forward and walked the aisle toward Amanda's future.

Chad stood tall and handsome beside his old high school friends, Kevin and Brad. He watched Kara at first, then his gaze lifted and he never looked away from Amanda. His smile grew the closer she came until her father joined their hands and stepped away.

Amanda couldn't have been happier as she exchanged vows with Chad. He kissed her with tenderness that spoke of his love. She responded with all her heart and whispered for his ears alone, "I love you, Chad. I never stopped loving you."

"Or I you." He lifted her hand and kissed her fingers. "I will love you always."

Together they turned to face their friends and family, as Pastor Mattson said, "May I present to you Mr. and Mrs. Chad Randall?"

TATER TOT CASSEROLE

This is easy enough for even a non-cook such as Chad to fix but still tastes great. We enjoy casseroles at our house because of ease in preparing, but also because of the variety. A little experimenting with ingredients may produce your own favorite recipe, or try this one the way my family does it and see what you think.

1 pound ground beef, cooked and drained
1 can mushroom soup
1 cup milk
1 pound shredded cheddar cheese
1 package frozen Tater Tots, baked according to directions

Layer large casserole dish with ground beef, soup, milk, and half the cheese. Mix together. Add Tater Tots and gently stir into meat mixture being careful to not smash Tater Tots. Sprinkle remaining cheese over top. Preheat oven and bake for 15 minutes at 350 degrees or until cheese is melted.

A Letter To Our Readers

Dear Reader:

In order that we might better contribute to your reading enjoyment, we would appreciate your taking a few minutes to respond to the following questions. We welcome your comments and read each form and letter we receive. When completed, please return to the following:

Fiction Editor
Heartsong Presents
PO Box 719
Uhrichsville, Ohio 44683

1. Did you enjoy reading *Building Amanda's Future* by Mildred Colvin?

   ❑ Very much! I would like to see more books by this author!

   ❑ Moderately. I would have enjoyed it more if

   _____

   _____

   _____

2. Are you a member of **Heartsong Presents**? ❑ Yes ❑ No

   If no, where did you purchase this book? _____

   _____

3. How would you rate, on a scale from 1 (poor) to 5 (superior), the cover design? _____

4. On a scale from 1 (poor) to 10 (superior), please rate the following elements.

   ____ Heroine   ____ Plot

   ____ Hero   ____ Inspirational theme

   ____ Setting   ____ Secondary characters

5. These characters were special because? _____

_____

_____

6. How has this book inspired your life? _____

_____

_____

7. What settings would you like to see covered in future
   Heartsong Presents books? _____

_____

_____

8. What are some inspirational themes you would like to see
   treated in future books? _____

_____

_____

9. Would you be interested in reading other **Heartsong
   Presents** titles? ❏ Yes   ❏ No

10. Please check your age range:
     ❏ Under 18   ❏ 18-24
     ❏ 25-34   ❏ 35-45
     ❏ 46-55   ❏ Over 55

Name _____

Occupation _____

Address _____

City, State, Zip_____

E-mail _____

WOLFSBANE

Demolitions expert Danielle Roark has been left behind in hostile territory during a mission with Nightshade. Former Green Beret and medic Canyon Metcalfe, beset with memories of another mission gone bad, vows to rescue her, sacrificing everything. As secrets unravel, will Canyon and Dani find healing, closure, and each other?

Romance, paperback, 352 pages, 5.5" x 8.375"

Please send me _____ copies of *Wolfsbane*. I am enclosing $12.99 for each.
(Please add $4.00 to cover postage and handling per order. OH add 7% tax.
If outside the U.S. please call 740-922-7280 for shipping charges.)

Name _____

Address _____

City, State, Zip_____

To place a credit card order, call 1-740-922-7280.
Send to: Heartsong Presents Readers' Service, PO Box 721, Uhrichsville, OH 44683

Heart♥ng

GET MORE FOR LESS FROM YOUR CONTEMPORARY ROMANCE!

Buy any assortment of six *Heartsong Presents* titles and save 25% off the already discounted price of $3.99 each!

Any 6 **Heartsong Presents** titles for only $20.95*

*plus $4.00 shipping and handling per order and sales tax where applicable. If outside the U.S. please call 740-922-7280 for shipping charges.

HEARTSONG PRESENTS TITLES AVAILABLE NOW:

___HP729 *Bay Hideaway*, B. Loughner
___HP730 *With Open Arms*, J. L. Barton
___HP754 *Red Like Crimson*, J. Thompson
___HP758 *Wedded Bliss*, K. Y'Barbo
___HP762 *Photo Op*, L. A. Coleman
___HP785 *If the Dress Fits*, D. Mayne
___HP786 *White as Snow*, J. Thompson
___HP789 *The Bride Wore Coveralls*, D. Ullrick
___HP790 *Garlic and Roses*, G. Martin
___HP806 *Out of the Blue*, J. Thompson
___HP814 *The Preacher Wore a Gun*, J. Livingston
___HP817 *By the Beckoning Sea*, C. G. Page
___HP821 *Clueless Cowboy*, M. Connealy
___HP830 *The Bossy Bridegroom*, M. Connealy
___HP834 *Salt Water Taffie*, J. Hanna
___HP838 *For the Love of Books*, D. R. Robinson
___HP865 *Always Ready*, S. P. Davis
___HP885 *A Hero for Her Heart*, C. Speare & N. Toback
___HP886 *Romance by the Book*, M. Johnson
___HP889 *Special Mission*, D. Mayne
___HP890 *Love's Winding Path*, L. Bliss
___HP893 *Disarming Andi*, E. Goddard
___HP894 *Crossroads Bay*, K. Kovach
___HP897 *Polar Opposites*, S. P. Davis
___HP898 *Parting Secrets*, B. Melby & C. Wienke
___HP901 *Gaining Love*, J. Johnson
___HP902 *White Roses*, S. T. Vannattes
___HP905 *Boxed into Love*, C. Speare & N. Toback

___HP906 *Perfect Ways*, J. Odell
___HP909 *Portrait of Love*, D. Mayne
___HP910 *Where the Dogwoods Bloom*, M. Johnson
___HP913 *Exposing Amber*, G. Goddard
___HP914 *Heart of Mine*, L. Bliss
___HP917 *Pure Serendipity*, B. Melby & C. Wienke
___HP918 *Fine, Feathered Friend*, K. Kovach
___HP921 *White Doves*, S. T. Vannatter
___HP922 *Maid to Love*, J. Johnson
___HP925 *Mending Fences*, C. Speare & N. Toback
___HP926 *The Thing about Beauty*, D. Robinson
___HP929 *Facing Tessa's Past*, M. Colvin
___HP930 *Wasatch Love*, L. Bliss
___HP933 *Praying for Rayne*, E. Goddard
___HP934 *Lily of the Field*, R. R. Zediker
___HP937 *White Pearls*, S. T. Vannatter
___HP938 *Betting on Love*, J. Johnson
___HP941 *In the Cool of the Evening*, J. Spaeth
___HP942 *Peace, Be Still*, T. Fowler
___HP945 *Perfect Peace*, J. Odell
___HP946 *Redeeming Sarah's Present*, M. Colvin
___HP949 *Canyon Walls*, J. Jarnagin
___HP950 *Shades of the Past*, D. Mayne
___HP953 *No One but You*, D. Robinson
___HP954 *Game of Love*, J. Johnson
___HP957 *Sunshine*, J. Spaeth
___HP958 *Plainsong*, D. Franklin

(If ordering from this page, please remember to include it with the order form.)

⸻ Presents ⸻

Great Inspirational Romance
at a Great Price!

Heartsong Presents books are inspirational romances in contemporary and historical settings, designed to give you an enjoyable, spirit-lifting reading experience. You can choose wonderfully written titles from some of today's best authors like Wanda E. Brunstetter, Mary Connealy, Susan Page Davis, Cathy Marie Hake, Joyce Livingston, and many others.

When ordering quantities less than six, above titles are $3.99 each.
Not all titles may be available at time of order.

SEND TO: **Heartsong Presents** Readers' Service
P.O. Box 721, Uhrichsville, Ohio 44683
Please send me the items checked above. I am enclosing $ _____
(please add $4.00 to cover postage per order. OH add 7% tax. WA add 8.5%). Send check or money order, no cash or C.O.D.s, please.
To place a credit card order, call 1-740-922-7280.

NAME _____

ADDRESS _____

CITY/STATE _____ ZIP_____

HP 8-11

HEARTSONG
PRESENTS

If you love Christian romance…

$12.⁹⁹

You'll love Heartsong Presents' inspiring and faith-filled romances by today's very best Christian authors…Wanda E. Brunstetter, Mary Connealy, Susan Page Davis, Cathy Marie Hake, and Joyce Livingston, to mention a few!

When you join Heartsong Presents, you'll enjoy four brand-new, mass-market, 176-page books—two contemporary and two historical—that will build you up in your faith when you discover God's role in every relationship you read about!

Mass Market 176 Pages

Imagine…four new romances every four weeks—with men and women like you who long to meet the one God has chosen as the love of their lives…all for the low price of $12.99 postpaid.

To join, simply visit www.heartsong presents.com or complete the coupon below and mail it to the address provided.

✂ -

YES! Sign me up for Heartsong!

NEW MEMBERSHIPS WILL BE SHIPPED IMMEDIATELY! Send no money now. We'll bill you only $12.99 postpaid with your first shipment of four books. Or for faster action, call 1-740-922-7280.

NAME _____

ADDRESS_____

CITY_____ STATE _____ ZIP _____

**MAIL TO: HEARTSONG PRESENTS, P.O. Box 721, Uhrichsville, Ohio 44683
or sign up at WWW.HEARTSONGPRESENTS.COM**